Published in

Copyright ©

The author o   nder the
Copyright, Designs and Patents Act, 1988, to be
identified as the author or authors of this work.

All Rights reserved. No part of this publication may be
reproduced, copied, stored in a retrieval system, or
transmitted, in any form or by any means, without the
prior written consent of the copyright holder, nor be
otherwise circulated in any form of binding or cover
other than that in which it is published and without a
similar condition being imposed on the subsequent
purchaser.

Praise for Gail Jones

<u>Family Secrets</u>

A heartwarming and realistic story, once I started I couldn't put it down. Ideal book for 12+.'   Melissa

'Family Secrets' is a really imaginative and eventful book. It's absolutely great for teenagers. Especially because of the emotions and how realistic the characters are! Jade yr7

<u>Family Fear</u>

This is an enthralling storyline and the way the writer captures the personality of the characters is amazing. Once I started reading I couldn't put the book down.   Christina – 12-year-old bookworm!

Can't wait for 'Family Missing' to come out, I've read 'Family Fear' and 'Family Secrets'! Best books I've read, :) Sophie aged 11

<u>Family Missing</u>

Great story with plenty of suspense. Ellen aged 15

The book was really cool. It's a whirlpool of adventures going on all over the place. Hania aged 13

<u>Witness</u>

I really enjoyed reading Witness, I felt that it was fast paced. Which made me enjoy it more. Hadassah aged 13

I think Witness is a fantastic story. I couldn't put it down. Cody aged 14

Index

Praise for Gail Jones

Chapter one – A Weird Day
Chapter two – Bruises
Chapter three – Emma
Chapter four – Really?
Chapter five – Last Chance
Chapter six – Rescue
Chapter seven – Police
Chapter eight – Lisa
Chapter nine – Suspicions
Chapter ten – Boyfriend
Chapter eleven – Liam
Chapter twelve – Regrets
Chapter thirteen – Problems
Chapter fourteen – Fall Out
Chapter fifteen – Mission
Chapter sixteen – Gone
Chapter seventeen – Against Time
Chapter eighteen – Collision
Chapter nineteen – Eli

Acknowledgements

Other books by Gail Jones

Contact Gail Jones

CHAPTER ONE – A WEIRD DAY

"You can't do that!" I stared at Leah, ignoring a cheer from the boys playing basketball behind her.

"But I have to!" Leah's eyes were red and moist as she sat on the grassy slope.

I leaned forward, hands on hips.

"What part of 'your body, your choice' don't you understand?"

"But he'll dump me." Leah's frown deepened. She twisted her hands, wringing them like a damp cloth.

"Who says?"

"Jake says." She glanced around to make sure no one could hear. "He says unless I, you know, then I don't love him and he might as well get somebody else."

"Bull!" Standing lower down the slope I was almost at eye level with my friend.

"No, it's true, that's what he said!" Leah chewed her bottom lip. "I can't lose him, Jess, I just can't."

I sighed. "Listen, Leah. I know you love him but that line is as old as my grandmother. If he loved you he'd be willing to wait. Don't let him talk you into something you don't want to do."

"Oh, I don't know." Leah's head dropped. "I wish I was as confident as you."

"Me? I'm not confident. I doubt myself all the time but nobody's gonna make me do something I don't want to, that's all. Look, just promise me you'll think about it and not rush into it. Okay?"

As the bell rang for registration, Leah looked at me and nodded. "Okay."

I led the way in for what would become a rubbish and weird day. Actually, the weird part started before I even arrived at school. I was walking along Haugh Road when I spotted a boy. Okay, yeah, there were lots of boys, all in uniform, heading towards the gates, and a day of torture, but this boy was different. He was about fifteen or sixteen and leaning casually against the school railings. He wore jeans and a grey hoodie with the hood down, revealing brown hair swept over his forehead. His face was perfect, handsome without being girly, with big brown eyes like chocolate and he was looking down the road, towards me. I knew he couldn't be looking at me, he had to be waiting for his girlfriend or something. As I walked nearer, I was tempted to stop and mess with my mobile, pretending to check messages, so I could ogle him a bit more and maybe snap a photo but I quickly dismissed the idea. With my luck, he'd figure out what I was doing and I'd be mortified.

A couple of lads were coming up behind me, their long legs out striding mine; maybe he was waiting for them? But no, they walked straight past. I felt my cheeks heat up when I realised those brown eyes were actually focussed on me.

But why? Someone that gorgeous wouldn't be interested in me, unless ... I glanced down then reached behind me and relaxed when my fingers confirmed my skirt wasn't tucked into my knickers. *So why is he looking at me? There's no way he fancies me, no boys fancy me, especially one this gorgeous.*

I was really close to him now and not sure where to put my eyes; his constant gaze made me feel uncomfortable and I wished he'd just look away, even for a second. Part of me wanted to stare back but I didn't want him to see me doing it. As I drew level, I focussed ahead feeling his eyes follow me.

"Hi."

My heart nearly stopped. *He's actually speaking to me!*

I looked around just to make sure he wasn't talking to anyone else, but no, there was no one else near enough.

"Hi," I said.

"Everyone gets to your school early."

I shrugged. "Boys play football, girls talk."

Yep, real mine of wisdom, that's me.

"It's good. Everyone gets to mine at the last minute."

"Which school is that?"

"It doesn't matter."

Oka-ay, so he doesn't want to share.

"Today's going to be tough but it'll work out better than it seems," he said.

Huh? What's this, a Chinese proverb or something?

"Ri-ight."

"See you later, Jess."

"Yeah, see you …" *Did he just use my name*?

I was about to ask how he knew me but he'd already pushed away from the railings and was walking away, back down Haugh Road.

Well, that was weird.

By the time I'd finished advising Leah I'd just about pushed mystery boy from my mind; I mean, let's face it, the chances of seeing him again when he didn't actually go to my school were, like, nil. Although, his perfect face jumped to the front of my mind more times than I could count that day but I kept pushing him away.

After my usual struggle with History, Biology and French, I walked into the dining hall, or café as we call it, ready to rest my frazzled brain and feed my gurgling stomach.

My friends stood with me, our trays full, scanning the room. The long, grey tables with little round stools facing the food bar were full, so were the smaller tables with four fixed chairs on the extreme right and left. The only ones left were on the other side of the walkway, tucked at the back of the room, behind a row of columns. Leah and Tammy went through the gap and walked half way along to sit behind the long table and across from me and Queenie.

There I was, perched on my stool, happily munching my chicken when Leah and Tammy's faces sagged. Their eyes focussed on something over my shoulder as a shadow cast over my food and a voice declared.

"That's my place. Move."

Well, maybe I'm just smart but I guessed straight away who it was and my stubborn streak kicked right in.

Leah and Tammy must have seen the signs and shook their heads at me. In the corner of my eye, I saw Queenie doing the same beside me. But did I take any notice? Did I heck.

Turning around, I looked into sixteen-year-old Lisa's, unfortunately, extremely beautiful face and said, "No."

That's it, that's all I said but it opened up a whole world of trouble.

A hush spread along the length of our table, and the one behind it, like a breeze and every head turned in our direction. Anybody would think I'd used a megaphone; the response was so quick. Even people across the walkway hushed, their attention focussed on us.

I realised I'd made a big mistake choosing this seat, not only was it right at the back but a wide column hid me from the sight of the dinner ladies.

"What did you say?" Lisa's piercing blue eyes shot lazerbeams at me while I sat up straight and tried to look confident.

"I said, 'No'. This is my seat and I'm not moving."

I could see my friends squirming. Usually, when Lisa picked on a person they moved and so did all their friends, so that her entourage could sit with her. It was either obey or suffer the consequences and Lisa had no limit to the punishments she could dream up. Unlike other bullies, her methods were usually pretty physical, no online bullying for Lisa, she was strictly hands-on. One day, some psychologist will have a real challenge trying to figure her out, I wish them luck, I've known her for three years now and still haven't managed it. The only thing I do know is that there's never any trace of her 'activities': a piece of torn up homework here, a punch in the stomach there, a vicious rumour somewhere else. Nothing could ever be traced back to her; victims never have the courage to speak up because they know worse will follow if they do and witnesses are threatened. Yep, one day she'll make a great mob boss.

My friends didn't know what to do. I could see glances flicking between them. If they moved they would be letting me down, but if they stayed they could be in as much trouble as me.

"Nobody says 'no' to me." Lisa's eyes dropped to my tray and her hand snapped out to grab it.

I saw her move, my brain switched off, and my instincts took over. I lashed out and knocked her arm away.

A universal gasp issued from everyone within viewing distance. I'd done the unthinkable, I'd actually struck Lisa. The alcove pulsed with expectation as every occupant on this and other nearby tables awaited my doom. I could even see heads leaning out, straining to see around the thick white column. I mean, they couldn't miss out on a bit of action, could they?

Lisa blinked at her three friends who immediately turned to the table behind them and pushed everyone's trays away. No one objected when they put down Lisa's and their own, freeing up their hands.

Now, any smart person would probably apologise at this stage and make a swift run for it but not me; smart is not my middle name. It's not that I'm brave, far from it, I'm just stubborn.

My brain did switch back on though and, after a moment's thought, I decided to stay sitting rather than stand and face them. This was for several reasons.

1. Sitting down, I was less of a target.
2. If a teacher came in, I would look like the innocent party (which I was).
3. Sitting gave me the moral high ground. Lisa was the aggressor, not me. This point wouldn't really do me much good but if I

was gonna get splattered it helped to at least know I was the better person.

Decision made, I sat looking up into four beautiful but very mean faces. In America they'd all be cheerleaders and rule the school. In Britain they're not cheerleaders but they still rule the school. All the boys fancy them and most of the girls (those who have wide hips, extra fat, undeveloped boobs, spots or generally consider themselves unattractive; in other words, most of us) want to be them. Just a pity they had their compassion and humanity surgically removed at birth.

My stomach resembled a cement mixer and I wished I hadn't actually eaten any chicken as the evil horde pounced. Lanky Melissa and got-to-be-a-boob-job Becky, (from here on known as: BJ Becky), unceremoniously dragged me to my feet. Lisa led the way while red-headed Alana trailed along behind.

"Why don't you all just grow a brain and realise violence doesn't solve anything?" I said, as their nails dug into my flesh. Lisa looked over her shoulder and smiled and it wasn't a nice one, more like a cat just before it snaps up the mouse.

"To the toilets."

Instantly, my stomach stopped churning and my food dropped right to the bottom like coke cans in a dispenser. My courage abandoned me and I was ready to beg. Lisa's command meant only one thing, they were going to implement the oldest school torture since toilets were invented. I was gonna have an early shower. Yes, I know totally extinct, right? Wrong. Told you there's something different about Lisa. One day I'll find out what and why but at that moment I just wanted to avoid a dunking.

"It's all right ladies," I said, trying humour. "I washed my hair this morning; I know it gets greasy quickly but eau de toilet is not my preferred washing style."

Lisa stuck her face a centimetre from mine.

"Hard luck. We're going to find the dirtiest toilet in the school and introduce you to it. Won't that be nice?"

A murmur spread around the hall. I knew what they were thinking.

'Should we do something, stay here or follow and watch?'

I might be fairly popular but a dunking's, a dunking. It's something everybody wants to see or gossip about but not experience. Anyway, to stop it they'd have to stand up against Lisa and the chance of that ever happening was, like, totally zero. Everyone knows that Lisa always pays back whoever crosses her, no matter how long it takes.

My feet scraped across the floor, my trainers squealing on the polished wood, as I tried to pull back but my efforts were useless.

We were now in full view of the food bar but the staff were serving, their heads barely visible over the huddle of students braying for food.

The café doors drew ever closer.

I could have shouted for help but then even more people would have seen my predicament and I wasn't exactly in the mood for publicity. Not to mention every bully in school thinking I'm weak or a snitch. Plus, Lisa would only get me double later. I was gonna have to take this, clean up quickly, then brazen it off and make people think it didn't bother me. There was no way I'd let anyone think of me as a wimp and an easy target. I might as well paint a bull's-eye on my back.

The doors clanked as Lisa pushed them open. She very kindly held them wide so her precious princesses could drag me out without losing their grip.

Small groups of year 7s clustered in the corridor and beneath the stairs even though their dining time ended twenty minutes ago. None of them moved to help, of course; they all knew what was going on and had the sense or lack of courage to do anything about it. They just gaped as I was dragged past.

One more metre and my fate would be sealed.

"What's going on here?"

Hands melted away and I nearly fell from the sudden lack of support. Waving my arms, I managed to regain my balance and looked up to where Mrs Quinn, the Math's teacher, stood tall and stern, halfway down the stairs.

"Nothing, Miss," Lisa said, her voice sweet and sickly.

"It doesn't look like nothing." Mrs Quinn was about the only teacher not taken in by Lisa's 'Miss-Goody-Two-Shoes' act.

"Jess?"

Oh boy, what an opportunity. I could open my mouth and get Lisa and co suspended but that wouldn't be the end of it. They'd be back and I'd be dead. So, reluctantly, I said.

"We were just playing, Miss."

"Well, take it outside," Mrs Quinn grunted, "And that goes for the rest of you. If you've eaten your lunch out you go."

About half the year 7s scuttled away but the rest still stood, apparently frozen, after their brief introduction to school violence.

"Out!"

Like a starting pistol the snapped word had instant effect and everyone scattered.

"Later," Lisa whispered in my ear before flicking her long, blonde hair over her shoulder and sashaying back to the café to retrieve her dinner. Her minions followed like ducklings behind their mother.

I stayed put; for some reason my appetite had vanished. Why did I have to be so pig-headed? If I'd just moved out of the way that would've been the end of it but no, not me, I had to open my big mouth. Now I was gonna have to watch my back all day because Lisa never left a 'debt' outstanding, her reputation depended on it.

Mrs Quinn descended the stairs as Leah, Queenie and Tammy burst from the café.

"Outside girls," she said, before turning the corner and disappearing from view.

"Jess, what happened?" Queenie's black, plaited extensions swung as she grabbed my arm.

"I thought you'd been dunked," Tammy said, looking me up and down and flicking her own blonde curls.

"Are you all right?" Leah asked, quietly, "I'm sorry we didn't help." Her brown eyes begged forgiveness.

I shrugged. "What could you do?"

Although, I've got to admit, it would've been nice if they'd stood up for me. I hadn't really expected it but, still, a girl likes to be surprised sometimes, especially when facing a dunking.

"So, what happened?" Tammy asked, still looking at my dry hair as though expecting droplets to burst out any minute.

"Mrs Quinn appeared and threw everyone out."
My friends grimaced in unison.

"You know it's not over?" Leah asked.

"They're gonna be so annoyed they didn't get to do it," Queenie added, "It's gonna be so much worse now."

"Yeah, Queenie, thanks for that," I said, "I really needed cheering up."

She shrugged. "Sorry."

We walked out into the sunshine and across the bottom yard where several groups stood chatting and others played basketball. We went down several cement steps then took our usual spot on the grassy slope beside them. Even though I knew her majesty was still at lunch I couldn't help looking around, my stomach twisting up like a badly tied shoe lace. Lisa was gonna get me; the only question was, when?

***

I spent the rest of the day waiting for the inevitable payback and as the final bell rang I was impatient to get away. Tammy has phys. Ed. last lesson every Monday and leaves via the Monkwood Road exit, nearest the gym, with her boyfriend, Dwaine.

My last lesson was at the opposite side of school so I walked across the staff car park with my other friends. At the gates Queenie gave me a friendly thump and turned right with her boyfriend of two years, Chad. Leah smiled and followed them with her uncaring, only wants one thing, boy-jerk, Jake. That left me, the girl with no boyfriend, to walk home pathetically alone. I've never had a boyfriend. Leah says it's because I frighten them off. I'm too opinionated, apparently. She has a point but I'm not gonna turn into some 'yes' girl just so a boy will go out with me. I am who I am and they can either take it or leave it. Unfortunately, most of them, well all of them actually, choose to leave it. But that's their loss. If a boy hasn't got the guts to go out with a girl with her own opinions then I'm not interested. I want a *man*.

Like him! Mystery boy was back and looking at me! Was he waiting for me?

Don't be stupid, Jess, like that would ever happen, he doesn't even know you. But he knew my name. So, do I walk towards him and say 'hi' or pretend I haven't seen him and wait for him to speak?

"Ah, there you are." Lisa's voice broke through my thoughts and I realised I'd made the fatal mistake of being so taken up with the handsome hoodie I'd forgotten to watch for prowling reptiles. Sorry, I shouldn't say that, it's an insult to reptiles.

Within a fraction of a second Lisa and co. swooped down like flies on a pile of ... never mind.

"Payback time." Lisa's mouth stretched into a smug smile. Maybe being beautiful and an evil queen didn't work for everyone but Lisa had it down to perfection.

In a pack, they steered me across the road and over to a gap in the fence. A lot of students used this earthy path, down the side of a farmer's field, as a shortcut to Parkgate, at the bottom of the hill. I slipped and slid as they pushed me down the steep and narrow slope to an open area at the bottom.

Before I dropped too far, I glanced back at hoodie, hoping for a rescue, but he still leaned in the same position, his arms crossed, watching. Yes, he was actually watching.

The open area was still a little too public for Lisa so she shoved me around a leafy hedge onto the farmer's field. Once there, we were totally obscured except for anyone standing right next to the fence on the roadside.

Already tensing, ready for the oncoming pain, I glanced up with one last hope of a reprieve and he was there. My heart lifted. He'd shout or do something to stop them, wouldn't he? But as the first fist rammed into my stomach, forcing all the air in my lungs to explode from my mouth, there was silence. He did nothing.

Well, there wasn't exactly silence; the immediate air was filled with my grunts and groans and the satisfied, but muted, laughter and jeers of the queen and her minions. I mean, Lisa couldn't make too much noise and draw attention to her sadistic behaviour, now could she?

Girls that beautiful should be ladylike, not psychotic bullies. Trouble is, nobody's told them and my body found out the hard way, not for the first time, either. I'd sampled Lisa's form of power-keeping before. Why couldn't they be into cyber bullying, like everyone else, then I'd just block them. Now don't get me wrong, if they were into cyber bullying, I'd probably wish they'd just hit me and get it over with. Conclusion? Bullying sucks, big time, and right now my body was really feeling it. I didn't just take it though, as pain exploded all over me, I fought back. Trouble was, that first punch had stolen all my oxygen and most of my energy as well.

I managed a couple of punches. Melissa's lip split in a very satisfactory way when it collided with my fist but, with four against one, my chances were slim. It was like trying to fight off a bunch of cats, their claws were everywhere, tearing and thumping from all sides. Within a minute, I was on my knees and hurting badly.

"All right, that's enough."

At Lisa's command they drew back, ebbing away like the tide, leaving me curled up on the floor. The punishment hadn't lasted long but it felt like an hour to me. My head pounded, my left eye throbbed and my stomach felt like it'd been kicked. It probably had, there'd been so many blows, I couldn't remember.

"Not a word, Hardwick, or you'll get worse and, next time, move when you're told."

Noted. But would I? Probably not. That stubborn streak could be really hazardous to my health.

"She split my lip." I heard Melissa moan as they walked away.

"Stop whining," Lisa snapped. "You shouldn't have let her and you'd better think up a good excuse for the teachers tomorrow. Usual silence, you got it?"

"Yes, Lisa."

If I wasn't hurting so much, I might have felt sorry for Melissa; it looks like Lisa's friends are bullied as much as the rest of us but, then, they do choose to hang around with her and do her bidding. I suppose they think the reflected power is worth it.

As their voices faded, I pushed myself painfully to my knees. I wasn't quite ready to try standing up yet. At least, despite it being mid-March, it hadn't rained for a few days and I was dusty but not covered in mud.

Closing my eyes, I tried to figure out whether any of the pain meant serious damage.

After a brief self-diagnostic I figured big bruises and stiff muscles were gonna be the only after effects. I opened my eyes and clocked a pair of not-so-white trainers, straight in front of me. My eyes travelled upwards past jeans, and a grey hoodie to the gorgeous face of Mr Hot.

He held out his hand. I ignored it and scrambled to my feet, grimacing as pain shot through my ribs, like a hot poker.

"Are you okay?" His voice was sooo sexy but it wasn't going to get him off the hook.

"Like you care!"

He frowned and looked down at his feet.

"I do care."

"Oh yeah? Sure. That's why you just stood up there and watched?" I nodded towards his old position by the fence. "Is that how you get your kicks, watching girls being beaten up? I guess it's a pretty rare sight, must have been entertaining for you."

"No, it wasn't but I couldn't interfere."

I snorted. "Yeah, right, Mr Brave. Well, see ya!"

Turning to march away, my brain screamed *but he's so hot!* Then answered, *Yeah, and yellow too.*

"Wait!" He caught my arm and spun me around.

"Get off me! Who do you think you are? Watching me get creamed then thinking you can order me around? Well, think again!"

I shook off his hand and marched towards the hedge.

"Jess! Wait! I'm sorry. I couldn't interfere; it had to happen. There's a reason, a real good reason …"

I kept on walking.

Hang on, he's using my name again. How does he know who I am?

"… somebody needs you!"

It was like a lasso had looped over my head and wrapped around my body. I stopped, mid-stride, my brain crying *keep going* but my heart asking, *who needs me?*

I turned back.

"All right, you've got thirty seconds. Talk fast and, while you're at it, tell me how you know my name."

"Okay, I work for some people who help others. I can't tell you much about them right now but if you decide to work with us, I can tell you more."

"Work with you? I'm at school. The uniform?" I pointed down at the black cardigan, white shirt, black, white and orange striped tie and extremely dusty black trousers.

Hoodie shook his head.

"That doesn't matter, your school attendance shouldn't be affected but you could help a lot of people."

"Like who? Do you work for a charity? Do you want me to collect for the Third World or something?" I've done that before, I love helping people, not to mention acting as agony aunt to all my friends.

Hoodie shook his head again and smiled, his brown eyes sparkling with enthusiasm.

"No, nothing like that. Sometimes people make decisions that affect their whole lives, even whether they live or die. The people I work for try to help people make the right choices to make their lives better or even to save them."

A gust of wind rustled the leaves in the trees behind me and a blackbird whistled a warning to some kids scrambling down the path while my heart tripped faster. To be able to save someone, to actually do it this time might make up for … but he wasn't making any sense and my head ached from the battering.

"How can they do that? How can they know what somebody's thinking? And who are 'they', anyway?" I winced as another pain shot through my ribs.

"I can't tell you how, yet, just that they can. Well, they don't know what people are thinking but they know a whole lot of stuff; enough to help people, and you can be part of that." His eyes latched onto mine and caught them like magnets. "Look. There's a girl, your age. Her dad beats her up. She needs to report him. If she doesn't, in four weeks time, he's going to beat her so bad she'll die."

My heart tightened but my aching head filled with questions.

"And you know this, how? Are you psychic or something? Because I don't believe in that stuff."

"No. Like I said, the people I work for know. I promise I'll explain how they do it if you decide to work with us."

I looked at him trying to figure out whether he'd just escaped from a secure facility or was actually serious. I mean, the men with the cosy white jackets might be just around the corner. Half of me wanted to walk away from this weirdo and never look back but the other half burned with curiosity. I mean, what if he was telling the truth? How exciting was that? But how could this be for real? Mystery boy looked normal enough, in fact, he looked better than normal but it all sounded a bit too weird to me.

"What's your name?"

"Eli."

"Short for Elijah?"

"No, just Eli."

"Oh." I studied him for a minute. "So, if I help you with this girl, you'll tell me all about the people you work for?"

"As much as I can."

I must be off my head for even listening to this guy.

But I was too intrigued to leave. If this girl needed help, I couldn't just walk away. Anyway, there was no harm in hearing more.

"I'm not getting in a car with you," I said, arms folded.

"We'll catch the bus."

Well, that was easy, if he was planning to molest me, or something, I figured he'd try harder on the car thing. And if he wanted to get me alone then he was out of luck 'cause that was *sooo* not going to happen!

"I'll meet you after school tomorrow," Eli said.

"Why tomorrow?"

He grinned. "You'll see."

He strode past, leaving me to watch his well-shaped rear disappear up the slope.

That was one really weird guy, mysterious, annoying and probably insane but I was drawn to him and not just physically. There was something about him that felt like it was meant to be. I already knew I'd be going with him tomorrow; my curiosity and need to help others was like this great big itch that just had to be scratched. The fact that he was totally hot might have had a bit to do with it as well but, one thing was certain, I wasn't going to let down my guard around him until he'd proved himself, one way or the other. And yes, I noticed, he never did explain how he knew my name.

***

CHAPTER TWO – BRUISES

The next morning, I looked in the bathroom mirror and groaned. I had the shiner to beat all shiners. My right eye was black and swollen. My bottom lip was twice as big as it should be and looked like I had a permanent sulk. Everything ached. One round bruise on each side of my ribs looked like eyes and a long one, right across my stomach, did an excellent impression of a slightly-gaping mouth.

It would've been funny if it wasn't so painful.

Now, I'm not exactly pretty on a normal day; my shoulder-length, brown hair is straight and lifeless and my medium-sized face, blue eyes and button nose are nothing special; but today, with all this damage, I needed a major make-over.

I plastered on makeup, blatantly ignoring the school's 'discreet makeup' rule, but the result wasn't good. I looked like a grease-painted circus performer. No amount of makeup was ever gonna cover that shiner. I just hoped the teachers didn't make me wash it all off because that would look *so* much worse.

Mum stood, hands on very slim hips, giving me this concerned look when I came down for breakfast.

"I still think I should ring the school, Sweetheart," she said. "Those girls shouldn't get away with this."

I shook my head.

"It's not worth it, Mum. They'd only get excluded for a while and when they came back they'd want revenge. The head would end up suggesting I change schools away from them but why should I? I don't want to leave my friends when it's only Lisa's band that bother me."

Anyway, I knew how to stop being beaten or having my head dunked. I just had to kiss her feet and jump when she said jump. Yeah, sure; global warming would end first.

"You would not be the one to leave school. Those girls would." Mum's wavy, brown hair swung about her shoulders as she worked herself up.

"Mum, it's okay. I'll sort it."

"How?" She gave me the thin-lipped 'prove it, Madam' look.

I sighed, we'd gone over the same ground last night and I didn't want to go there again. It'd taken me ages to talk her out of ringing school. At one point she even wanted to call the police!

I shrugged.

"I don't know yet, but I will. Okay?"

"No, it's not okay, you go to school to learn not get beaten up."

"Mum, it's only one idiot and her friends. I'll find a way to sort it. I have to fight my own battles."

I knew that would work, Mum was big on fighting your own battles. She visibly sagged as she gave in.

"All right, Sweetheart. I admire you for wanting to do that. But if this happens again I'm stepping in. Right?"

"Yes, Mum."

At least my brother, Jimmy, and ten-year-old sister, Abby, weren't at home or they would've joined in as well. Both were staying over at friends' houses. Yep, I know that's rare on a school night but both had good reasons. Abby had a joint project with her best friend Cassy and seventeen-year-old Jimmy was off on a field trip today with his class and his mate's dad was driving them to the station for a very early start.

Interrogation over, I was glad to get out of the house.

As soon as I turned onto Haugh Road, I scanned for Eli. When I didn't see him the heaviness in my chest doubled, but why?

Why do I want to see someone who watched me being beaten up? Okay, I admit it, because he's gorgeous and I'm intrigued with all the helping people stuff.

"Hey, Jess!"

Queenie was walking across the staff car park, towards me, from the entrance further up the road. I met her half way.

As soon as she saw me, she stopped and stared.

"When did they get you?"

"Straight after school."

Queenie frowned. "So that's why you missed guitar practice. I should have stayed with you; sorry."

With all that happened, I'd completely forgotten guitar practice. We both took lessons every Monday evening.

I shrugged.

"They would have gotten me eventually and, if you'd been with me, they might have got you too."

"Why do you have to wind Lisa up?" Queenie asked, "Why don't you just move when she tells you?"

"Because I'm not her slave and she can't order me about. Anyway, somebody's got to stand up to her."

Queenie's head dropped.

"I wish I was brave like you."

I grinned then winced when my lip hurt.

"Haven't you heard? I'm not brave, just stupid."

Queenie smiled, linked arms and marched me into school.

***

My last lesson before lunch was Maths. Mrs Quinn never lets anybody out when the bell rings; she always chooses that moment to announce our homework. I fidgeted, like my chair was riddled with ants, desperate to get in and out of the café before Lisa appeared. If she came in while I was eating she was bound to choose me to move again, just to make a point. I've defied Lisa over loads of things before and had my homework torn up, a punch in passing or some other punishment. But this time everyone witnessed my defiance so Lisa will keep at me until I publicly give in. Walking around sporting a black eye proves I've been punished but I also have to be seen to have learned my lesson and obey when she commands.

As soon as I finished scribbling down the homework I snatched up my books, stuffed them into my bag and was first to reach the door.

"Jess. I'd like to see you a moment." Mrs Quinn's voice rose above the clatter.

Groaning, I turned and allowed everyone to rush past me.

"Yes, Miss?"

"I cannot help but notice your eye and your lip. Does this have anything to do with the incident I witnessed yesterday?"

Perfect opportunity number two. To sprag or not to sprag, that is the question. Shakespeare would be proud.

"Erm, no Miss." Lisa should kiss my feet with gratitude. But will she? Will she heck. "Erm, it was somebody from another school. I broke up a fight on my way home."

Mrs Quinn gave me this, 'I don't believe a word of it', look.

"Jess, you must understand that bullies will continue to be bullies until someone stands up to them. Reporting them can make a difference."

Yeah, sure, I thought, *It can get me splattered even more quickly and effectively than normal.*

"Yes, Miss." Was what I actually said, "Can I go now, Miss?"

"I'll be keeping an eye on both of you," she said, "Bullying is not tolerated at this school but I can't do anything unless you speak up."

She had a point and maybe, one day, I'll be the one to speak up but for now I just stood there, silently urging her to let me go.

Mrs Quinn sighed, "You may go."

I got out of there fast before she could change her mind and ask more awkward questions.

Walking into the café made my stomach churn and it wasn't from hunger. I'd managed to avoid all sightings of Lisa and co. and didn't want that to change.

I chose toad-in-the-hole and carried my tray over to a table already occupied by my friends.

They looked up with strained smiles as I set down my tray and slid into the only empty seat. Our table was in the main part of the café and in full sight of the sandwich bar. It didn't take much imagination to work out why they'd picked this one.

"Hi," said Leah, a little quiver in her voice.

"Hi," said Tammy, not looking quite as bouncy as usual.

Queenie just grimaced. We all knew what could happen.

I ate every mouthful with an eye on the door. My throat felt so tight, it was like forcing my food down a funnel, but I still managed to finish in half the normal time. Everybody else was ready before me and as soon as I drained my water, and put down the empty beaker, Tammy spoke.

"Let's head outside. It's too hot in here."

She was right, it was roasting, but we all knew the real reason for her hurry and it had nothing to do with the temperature.

We stood, as one, and strode to the bins.

I was last in line and had just scraped in my waste when the doors swung open and Lisa strolled in.

She spotted me straight away and smirked.

"Finished already, Hardwick? My, didn't you eat quickly? Anybody would think you were in a hurry. I wonder why?"

I felt my cheeks burn but couldn't stop myself responding.

"I wanted to be out of here before you arrived," I said, watching a triumphant smile spread across her face, "Because looking at you makes me feel sick."

Lisa's smile dropped as Leah gasped.

"Don't push it, little Jess, you don't know who you're messing with," Lisa said before oozing to the front of the dinner queue and elbowing out those already waiting. A few of them muttered objections but no one kicked up a fuss as her crew slid in behind her.

"Wow, that was tense," Leah said, as we left the café and the doors clattered shut behind us.

"Why do you do it?" asked Tammy, "It's like you've got a death wish or something."

I shrugged. What could I say? Even I didn't know why I did it. I just couldn't help myself. It was like some built-in programming, or something, one look at Lisa and I got verbal diarrhoea.

***

Fortunately, I managed to avoid her for the rest of the day and called a cheery, "See ya!" to my friends as they all turned in the opposite direction, with their boyfriends.

I turned left and spotted Eli.

Wearing what looked like the same hoodie, Eli leaned against the railings a couple of metres in front of me.

Instantly, a hoard of grasshoppers danced a jig in my stomach while I silently ordered them to quit. I didn't want to be this glad to see him; he was too warped to be boyfriend material. But even my eyes betrayed me. They roved over his body, taking in the muscles pushing against his jeans and hoodie sleeves.

His head turned in my direction and fixed me with his warm, brown eyes.

I looked away, feeling my ears burn. He'd caught me checking him out; how embarrassing was that?

When I looked back at him, he wore a knowing smile. Boy, did he know he was hot!

Part of me wanted to walk the other way, to show I wasn't hooked, but he was like a fisherman reeling me in. I couldn't stop my feet heading towards him.

"You ready?" he asked, when I was a couple of strides away.

"Erm, yeah," I said, intelligently, my brain momentarily in meltdown at the sight of his face. "Where are we going?"

"I'll tell you on the way."

He turned and started walking, expecting me to follow, but I didn't. He'd taken several steps before realising I wasn't at his side.

"What's up?" he asked, turning his frown on me.

"I'm not a dog, a slave or a puppet. Okay? You don't say 'follow' and expect me to obey."

His mouth tweeked into an amused smile.

"Sorry. Would you like to join me, Jess?" He waved his arm with a flourish and bowed before checking his watch. "Our bus leaves in roughly four minutes."

"Okay, but don't try any funny business. I don't trust you. I'm just going to see what this is about then make up my mind."

Eli shrugged. "Fair enough, but can we get going?"

I gave a quick nod and caught up with him.

"So, are you gonna tell me what's going on?" I asked, struggling to keep up with his long strides.

"Like I said yesterday, there's this girl who needs to report her dad, like now, before it's too late."

"And how are we supposed to get her to do that?"

"Not we, you."

I stopped. "Me?"

Eli took a few more steps before realising I wasn't with him again. He turned and walked back to me, holding out a tissue.

"Wipe off most of your makeup then look in a mirror."

"What?"

Eli sighed. "Look, I know you've got all these questions but can you start walking please? The bus is gonna leave without us if we don't hurry up."

I pursed my lips, not a good idea when one of them is twice its normal size, and followed him.

At the end of the road we turned onto Blythe Avenue and reached the stop with seconds to spare.

Eli chose a middle seat away from some kids at the back and two old dears at the front. No one sat in the seats nearest us so, as the bus pulled out, Eli explained our mission.

***

CHAPTER THREE – EMMA

"The target's name is Emma Stone, known as Ems to her friends. She's fourteen, like you. Her mother, Mandy, left two years ago. She never spoke of it but our people think she was probably being beaten. Until that day, Matt Stone had never touched Emma so Mandy probably figured her daughter would be safe, and better off, with her father. She was wrong. Matt has been beating Emma ever since. Emma has never told anyone. Our mission is to make sure she does."

"How do you know all this? If she's never told anyone, how do the people you work for know about it? And you've never told me how they know she's gonna die in four weeks."

"Keep your voice down." Eli quickly scanned the other passengers before continuing in his hushed voice. "Look, I know all this seems unreal but it's the truth, honest. It's also a secret, if I told you about it right now you wouldn't believe me, but you will. Once you've met Emma, and can see I'm telling the truth, I can explain more. Then, if you decide to join us I'll explain everything, well, as much as I know, anyway."

"Yeah, right."

He had to be winding me up. If I wasn't such a Good Samaritan, I could just walk away but if there was even the slightest chance that any of it was real then I had to help Emma.

"So, if you know what's gonna happen, why can't I just tell her so she gets help?"

"How will you explain how you got your information 'Some boy I just met told me'? Do you really think she'll believe you?"

"Probably not, but if I can't tell her any of that then how can I persuade her to report her dad?"

"You're going to pretend the same thing happened to you but you spoke up and got help. Tell her you're safe now and she can be too."

"How am I supposed to do that? I don't know how she feels or what goes on when you ring for help. I don't even know who to ring."

"Tell her to ring Childline; and you do know how she feels."

"No, I don't."

"How have you felt about that bully all day?"

"I've avoided her like she's a vampire."

"No, not what you've done. How have you *felt*?"

I frowned. I wasn't into this 'bare all your feelings' stuff but Eli's intense eyes speared mine as though they were digging into my soul.

"I was scared, okay? I didn't want it to happen again so I stayed out of her way."

"Now imagine she lived at your house and you couldn't avoid her."

My stomach seized up at the thought.

"Now, what if she was your older sister who should love and care for you? Instead, one minute she's out to get you and the next she's really sorry and supporting."

I swallowed.

"I'd love her but hate how she treated me. I don't think I'd ever want to go home but where else would I go?" I looked at him as though seeing him for the first time. "That's why you let them hit me, isn't it? So I'd look the part and understand how she feels."

Eli nodded. "I'm sorry. I really wanted to wring their necks."

I smiled, maybe Eli wasn't so bad, after all.

I looked out the window while I processed everything; there was so much to take in. I didn't recognise any of the houses and suddenly realised I hadn't even taken note of what bus we were on or where we were going. Eli sounded sincere but if he wasn't I'd just put myself in a whole world of trouble. I wouldn't even know how to get home.

Reaching into my pocket I fingered my mobile, charged up last night, at least I had one lifeline.

"Oh flip, quick, duck down in your seat," he hissed.

"What?"

"You need to duck, for just a couple of minutes."

"No way!"

"Now, Jess!"

He pulled my arm, dragging me down.

"Get off me you pervert!"

The bus echoed with the sound of flesh against flesh as I slapped his cheek, hard. But he didn't let go. My head spun, sort of dizzy and fuzzy; had he given me something? But no, he couldn't have, I hadn't had a drink. There was nothing he could lace.

"We have to be down here," he said, his voice sounding crackly and broken up, like a phone with a poor signal. "I'm sorry, it's my fault, I should have warned you but I was too busy explaining everything else and only just realised where we were." He paused for a few seconds then, as the dizziness passed, he released my arm. "It's okay, you can sit up now."

I sat up abruptly and was about to push past him, and get off the bus, when something registered. Something was different, but what? I looked around as Eli sat up more slowly.

The front seats were empty. The bus had stopped a couple of times but I'd never noticed the old dears get off. A man sat two seats back on the opposite side of the bus. Where had he come from? I was pretty sure he hadn't passed us. The same kids were at the back but now there were only two of them. And where was the young mum with her baby, who got on a couple of stops ago?

I frowned at Eli whose smile would've made the Mona Lisa jealous.

"If you choose to join us, I'll tell you what just happened."

I glared at him, feeling my arm ache where he'd gripped me so tightly. His cheek glowed where I'd slapped him.

"Let me make one thing clear," I said, in my most commanding voice, "Don't ever touch me again, you understand? If you do, I'm out of here quicker than you can blink. You got that?"

"Yes, Jess." His voice sounded submissive but his eyes twinkled with amusement and did nothing for my temper. As the bus stopped, to take on more passengers, I fixed him with my fiercest look.

"This is not a joke. Yesterday you stood by and watched me get creamed. Today you grab me and pull me down in my seat. With your 'join us and I'll tell you why later' rubbish. Well, I'm telling you, there are no more chances, anything else I don't like and I'm gone. Okay?"

"We're here." Eli stood and pressed the red stop button. A 'ping' sounded from the front and seconds later the bus swerved into a stop.

I pulled myself up and followed him. And yes, I'd noticed he'd not answered me.

I stepped down off the bus and shivered. It was several degrees colder than when we set off so I pulled my coat tight around me, hugging myself to keep in the warmth.

"Emma will be sitting on a swing in that park," Eli said, pointing across the road. "She puts off going home as long as she can."

I gave him another 'how can you know that?' look and stepped to the curb. Aware of a gap at my shoulder, I looked back.

"Aren't you coming?"

"No, she won't trust me."

That figures, I thought. It was about the only understandable thing he'd said.

Suddenly my stomach twisted and I turned back. "This isn't some sort of trap, is it?"

Eli frowned.

"Lisa's set this up, hasn't she? You're in it with her! I'm so stupid! I mean, you knowing the future and all that. I'm such an idiot. She's in that park, right now, ready to record me on her phone and send it to the whole school, isn't she? I can see the text now: 'Jess, so desperate to be a 'goody-two-shoes' she actually believes someone can know the future.'" I shook my head. "What was I thinking? I'm going home."

Obviously, somebody as gorgeous as Eli wouldn't want anything to do with 'plain Jane' me. Lisa had played me like a hockey puck, right into her net. Tomorrow it'll go viral – without her name attached, of course. This was her way of showing me up in front of everybody and putting me in my place.

I scanned the other side of the road for a bus stop to take me home.

"Jess? What are you talking about? Who's Lisa? This is about Emma. She needs you. This is for real. If you don't help Emma, there's nobody else."

"There's loads of people."

"No, there isn't. There aren't many who care enough about others, are the right age, good at listening and giving advice, and live near enough to me. And I doubt many of those are covered in bruises, right now."

"So, go beat somebody up."

Cars whizzed past on the road behind me as I faced him, my arms folded.

His frown had deepened, cutting dark lines between his eyes.

"Please, Jess. She really needs you. You know you want to help her."

His face looked sincere enough but sociopaths are supposed to be hard to read. I didn't know what to do. One part of my brain yelled for me to get out of there fast and the other to believe him and stay.

I sighed.

"Okay. I'll go see but, I'm telling you, one sign of Lisa and that's it. I'm gone, for good."

"Okay." Eli nodded, "Oh, and Jess."

I waited.

"Don't mention the date."

"Why not?"

"I'll explain later if…"

"… if I decide to join you," I finished.

Eli grinned. "You're getting it."

I grimaced, turned back to the road, waited until it was clear then crossed over.

I walked through a narrow opening in the metal fence and scanned the park. A wide area of grass stretched out in front of me. Over on the right, a children's play area held swings, two slides, a climbing frame and a couple of bouncy kids' rides, made to look like horses. There was no sign of Lisa and co.

A mum shouted encouragement to her young son on the slide and a girl, about my age, rocked slowly on one of the swings. Even if the park had been full, I'd have known that was Emma. She sat, in a warm black coat, with her arms looped loosely around the chains and her toes on the floor, rocking aimlessly. Her head hung low and her long, blonde hair fell forwards, hiding her face. She looked so sad and alone. Just seeing her made me glad I'd come. Could she really be dead in a month if I didn't help her?

Chewing my lip, I walked across the grass wishing I hadn't been so suspicious and had thought to ask Eli what to say, not that he'd have been much help. He was real good at not saying much. Meanwhile, I hadn't a clue what to do. I might be good at advising my friends about everyday stuff but I knew them and this was a lot more serious.

The low gate on the children's play area creaked as I opened it. Emma didn't look up.

I chose the swing next to her and gently rocked.

Okay, what do I do now? Do I speak or just sit here?

In the end, I decided to just wing it. I didn't really have much choice.

"Hi, I'm Jess."

Emma didn't speak.

"I just moved here."

No response.

"What's your name?"

Still nothing, it was like I wasn't even there. I seriously doubted she could even hear me.

"Do you go to school around here? Only, I might be changing schools soon and I don't know anybody."

She continued rocking, her head still down.

The chains on the swings were so cold, my fingers felt like they were glued to them. I rubbed my hands together then slipped them into my pockets.

"Can you hear me?"

Her head lifted, "Look, no offence but …" She paused, studying my face.

"What happened to you?"

"About the same as happened to you, I reckon," I said, seeing a black eye through her makeup.

"I doubt it." Her head went down again.

Well done, Jess, you've just won first prize in 'how to lose someone's attention'.

"Erm, I don't really talk about it, but … no, never mind," I said, sounding as hesitant as I felt.

Her head came up again. "What?"

I shook my head. "It doesn't matter."

Gently, Jess, you've got her interest again.

Her eyes raked over my face as though trying to read something there.

"Who hit you?" she asked, eventually.

I shrugged.

Now, it was my turn to drop my head. It wasn't just play-acting either. I didn't want to lie to her and was sure she'd read the truth if she saw my face.

We sat in silence, my stomach wrapping itself in knots. I watched her feet slow down and finally settle. Would she get up and leave? Had I played this all wrong?

"Was it someone at school?" she asked, at last, her voice so soft I could barely hear her.

"No," I lied.

"Someone in your family?"

I nodded, wishing I could cross my fingers without her seeing me.

"Your brother?"

"I don't have one," I lied again.

"Your sister?"

I shook my head.

"Your mum?"

"No, my mum's great. Well, yeah, she is." I hesitated; to make my circumstances match Emma's, I had to pretend not to have seen my mum for years. Would I be living with her if taken from my dad or would I be in foster care? I had absolutely no idea.

"You're not sure?"

"Well, erm, I haven't seen her for years but she was always okay before … and I might be living with her again, soon."

"Because of your bruises?"

I nodded.

She was edging around it and so was I. The last thing I wanted was to frighten her off by being too direct.

"Did she ask you to live with her?"

"She doesn't know about it yet. They're trying to find her."

"Who?"

"Social Services."

I hoped I'd got that right. A girl in my tutor group was in foster care and I'd heard her mention Social Services.

"Doesn't your dad want you?" she asked, quietly.

"Oh yeah, but, you know."

I hung my head, hoping she'd figure out what I meant. I had no real experience of abuse but, if my dad was hitting me, I don't think I'd spell it out.

"Did your dad do that to your face?"

I nodded. We'd got there, at last, now I had to be convincing but it would be hard. My dad left when I was four-years-old and I've only seen him a couple of times since. He has a new family, a wife and two kids, and lives in America. Me, Jimmy and Abby are lucky to get birthday and Christmas cards. He left just after Abby was born, said he'd met someone and fallen in love. Great, hey?

"But he didn't mean to." I surprised myself but was sure if my dad really had hurt me I'd want to convince myself he didn't mean it and maybe he wouldn't, not really.

"Sometimes it just happens," Emma whispered.

"Yeah."

I finally looked up.

"Did your dad do that?" I nodded towards her and she nodded back.

"Does he do it a lot?"

She nodded again. "But not all the time," she said, quickly. "And only when I'm bad."

My throat twisted. I'd seen enough TV shows to know that victims often think it's their fault. Right then I wanted to thump her father in the eye and see how he liked it.

"Maybe it's not your fault," I said, softly.

The swing beside me groaned as Emma started rocking again. She was quiet for so long I was sure she disagreed with me.

"Maybe," she said, at last.

"Have you ever asked for help?" I asked, biting my lip and hoping I hadn't pushed too far.

"No."

Woa, that was decisive. This isn't going to be easy.

"Why not?" I looked at the ground again, not wanting my direct stare to unnerve her.

"Well, you can't, can you?"

"I did," I whispered.

I heard her gasp.

"What happened?"

"They got me out. I've just moved in with foster parents. That's why they're trying to find my mum."

Emma's silence was like a solid object beside me; only the squeak of the swing let me know she was still there.

"What's it like?" she said, at last.

I shrugged. How could I know? I tried to imagine how I'd feel if this was real.

"Scary," I said, "But home was scary too."

"I get scared a lot," she said, quietly.

I wanted to wrap my arms around her and promise to protect her but what could I really do?

"Maybe, you could get help too?"

"No." Emma's voice was strong again. "I couldn't."

Suddenly she was on her feet. She snatched up her black school bag from the floor beside her swing and walked away from me.

"Wait, please!"

But she didn't, she set off running and before I could get through the little gate she was clear across the park.

What did I say? How did I mess up?

A huge weight settled in my stomach.

She'd gone. I might never see her again. She would die because I hadn't saved her.

I hurried out to the road and found Eli pacing beside the entrance.

"What happened?" he demanded. "She ran out of there like a rabid dog was chasing her. What did you say?"

"Hey!" Before my brain engaged, I swung at him, giving his arm a hard thump.

"Hey, what's that for?" he said, massaging his arm.

"Don't you start blaming me! I'm the learner here and you didn't help at all. I don't know what I'm doing; I had to make everything up. When I help my friends I never have to lie because I already know them and what's going on with them. Lying just makes everything complicated. I've never been abused or known anyone who was. I was totally winging it. If I've messed up, I don't know how. We were talking but when I mentioned telling someone about it, she legged it. I couldn't stop her. And now she's going to die because I failed."

My eyes stung so I looked away.

"It's okay."

"No, it's not! I've never done anything like this before and Emma's nice; she deserved somebody better than me. I've let her down."

"No, you haven't."

"Yes, I have."

Eli took my chin and turned my face towards him.

"No, you haven't," he said, slowly. "Are you going to join us, Jess?"

"I don't know."

"I know this was hard, but you haven't failed, not yet anyway."

"I can try again?"

"If you decide to join us, yes. I can explain all the weird stuff then, as well."

"Like what?"

I knew what I'd found weird but wanted to know how much he was willing to explain.

"Like, disappearing bus passengers, why we had to duck in our seats and why you'll find something strange with your watch when we get back."

I examined my watch, it looked perfectly normal to me.

I sighed. What was I supposed to do? I wanted to help Emma but talking to her had been so hard. And what if I failed, again? The responsibility was huge!

"I don't know," I whispered.

Eli nodded.

"Look, think about it. I'll meet you tomorrow after school. There's one thing you should know, though; you are Emma's only chance."

"Why am I her only chance?"

"Because it'd be pretty suspicious someone else turning up all bruised with the same story and coming up with a different angle would be hard. Someone's already tried to reach her dad and failed, I don't think there'll be many more chances."

We hardly spoke on the way back to Rawmarsh. Eli had me do the silly slide-down-in-the-seat again but this time he gave me plenty of warning and just laid his hand gently on mine. Was it an excuse to touch me? But why? I wasn't much of a catch. But if it wasn't that then what was the reason? I couldn't figure it out and 'Mr Secrets' wasn't about to tell me anytime soon.

When I sat up, I noticed a mother and baby had left the bus without me seeing them and a single woman had taken the seat in front of us.

I looked at Eli. My face must have had a huge question mark painted on it because he just grinned and said, "Tomorrow."

"Eli," I started, as we arrived back on Blythe Avenue, "Can't you tell me anything?"

"Not until you decide. Tomorrow, Jess Hardwick." He smiled, turned and walked away.

I stood and watched him go. I'd never met such an annoying but strangely magnetic boy in all my life.

***

CHAPTER FOUR – REALLY?

The next day I learned nothing in school. My head was filled with thoughts of Emma and mysterious Eli, there was no room for anything else.

Part of me felt it had to be a dream. It was so weird with disappearing bus passengers and a girl needing my help; not to mention my watch playing up, just as Eli said it would. When I looked at it, late last night, it was eighty minutes fast. I've no idea why.

Another part of me knew that everything had really happened and felt equally excited and scared. This was the most important thing I'd ever been involved in; packed with responsibility, maybe more than I could handle, but if I could help enough people it might take away my hurt from failing … I pushed the thought away, I had enough to think about with Emma and Eli. I couldn't let my mind get tangled up with things I couldn't change. Fortunately, I didn't run into Lisa, for once; she would have tipped me over the edge.

"What's wrong with you today?" Queenie asked, as we crossed the car park, after school. "It's like you've had a lapotomy."

"A Lobotomy," I corrected.

"Yeah, whatever."

"You've got to admit, you're like a walking zombie," Tammy said. "I don't think you'd notice if Lisa came up and slapped you in the face."

"Er, yeah, I'd notice that."

As soon as we reached the gates, I looked around and spotted Eli. He was casually leaning against the railing in the same position as the day before. My friends followed my gaze.

"Oh, now I get it," Tammy said, grinning. "Jess is in love."

"No, I'm not." My face burned, knowing Eli was close enough to hear every word.

"Yeah, sure," Queenie said. "Your head's been on 'vacant' all day then your eyes jump out and stick like magnets to Mr Cool over there."

"Shh!" I hissed. This was so embarrassing. No way was I in love with 'weird guy of the month'. "I'm not in love; I'm just distracted."

"Yeah, and we know who by." Tammy smirked and let her eyes travel appreciatively over Eli. "I wouldn't mind a bit of that. If you get fed up, let me know and I'll step in. See you tomorrow and don't do anything I wouldn't do."

She winked before turning away. It's a good job all the boyfriends were at football practice or she'd be in trouble for that comment.

"He's hot," Leah whispered in my ear, "Nearly as hot as Jake."

Okay, now I feel sick.

"See you tomorrow," Leah said, "Then you can tell me all about him."

"There's nothing to tell," I called after her as she ran to catch up with the others.

Actually, there was a lot to tell but nothing that made any sense.

Still feeling hot, I walked slowly over to Eli and forced myself to look directly at him.

He hadn't moved but his smile said he'd heard every word and it didn't bother him at all.

"Nice friends," he said, while my cheeks burned even hotter. "So, Jess. What have you decided?"

"I'm going to join you," I said, surprising myself. Up to that moment I hadn't made a decision. I held my breath, expecting a drum roll or the earth to open, but Eli just smiled, revealing beautifully white teeth. Why was everything about him so perfect?

"Good," he said, standing sharply. "Let's walk and talk."

"Are we going to see Emma?"

"Not today, but it'll be harder for people to hear what we say if we walk."

I looked quickly around.

"Why, is someone spying on us?"

He laughed. "No, but we are talking about secret things."

"Oh, yeah."

Will I ever stop making myself sound like an idiot?

He looked down at me, staring at my face like it was the first time he'd seen it.

"What?"

"It's your bruises; they're showing through your makeup."

Great, now he thinks I look a mess; it's him who wanted the bruises, in the first place!

"When we go again, they need to be covered up."

"Why? I thought I had these for a reason."

"You had. They were for the last visit. The next time it should look like they're gone."

"Why?"

"Didn't you figure out what happened yesterday?"

"Yeah, I messed up but I'm guessing that's not what you're talking about."

"No, it isn't." Eli started walking towards Blythe Avenue and I followed. "Yesterday, when we travelled on the bus, we were transported in time."

"Is this a new service from Yorkshire Traction?" I laughed then stopped when I realised he wasn't laughing. "You're kidding, right?"

Eli shook his head. "The agency I work for can transport people in time. One of the ways is while we're travelling in a vehicle, such as a bus, but it can be when we're just standing somewhere. The problem with being out in the open is…"

"We can be seen."

"Exactly. Yesterday, we had a set location where that transfer would happen and at that point …"

"We ducked down in our seats."

He smiled. "Yeah, we ducked in our seats and I held your arm. While we were connected, we transported to the same bus two months earlier."

"No way!"

"It's true."

I stared at him as pieces slotted into place.

"That's why the other passengers changed! I wondered why I hadn't seen the old timers get off and the man get on; we weren't even on the same bus!"

"That's right and we bobbed down so no one would see us disappear or appear right in front of them."

"But what if people were sitting in our seats two months earlier? We'd end up on their laps."

Eli laughed. "That'd be fun."

"No, but seriously, what if that happened? Could we end up merged with their bodies or something? I've read books where that happened."

"That's fiction. I don't know exactly how the agency does it but they said something about a test that helps them work out whether a person is already in that location. They always tell me exactly where to sit so I suppose it's all worked out. When they don't use a bus, they tell me when and where to stand so they can pick me up."

"But how do they pin-point you on a moving bus?"

"They use the GPS from my phone to get my exact position. Don't ask me how they do that from the future; I'm no good at science and all this stuff goes straight over my head, so that's the best explanation I can give you. All I know is that my phone has to be on and the GPS working. You know what GPS is, don't you?"

I rolled my eyes. "Well, yeah. I am from this century. It stands for Global Positioning Satellite."

"Okay, so they use that to locate me then transport me and anyone I'm in physical contact with."

"That's why you held my hand?"

Why did my heart sink at that news? No way did I want this guy to fancy me. No way.

"Yeah, that's why." Eli nodded but his eyes twinkled; was there something he wasn't telling me?

A rogue part of me hoped there was.

Just at that moment, a switch clicked on in my brain.

"I think I've just figured out why my watch was wrong."

"Go on …"

"We travelled back in time, had our meeting, and on the journey back to Rawmarsh they returned us to the same time we'd set out from. For us eighty minutes had passed but for everyone else no time at all."

Eli grinned. "Yep, that's right. I couldn't tell you to alter your watch without telling you about time travel."

"And you couldn't tell me about that until I decided to join you."

Eli nodded.

Wow.

"Wait a minute; you said they're in the future, you know, the people in charge of the time travelling stuff. Have you met them? What are they like?"

"No, I've never seen them. I have a 'go-between' who passes on information and answers my questions, well, most of them, anyway."

"Who's your 'go-between'? Can I see him or her?" I looked around half expecting to see someone following us.

"Maybe." Eli shrugged. "Usually the 'go-between' only contacts one person in a team."

"Why?"

Eli shrugged again. "I think the less we all know about anyone else who works for the agency, the easier it is for them to keep it all a secret. I'll ask Zac if you can meet him."

"Is Zac your go-between?"

"Yes."

"So, are there people disappearing off buses and appearing on others all over the place?"

Eli grinned.

"No, there aren't many of us Time Fixers."

"Why not?"

"It's a small agency."

We'd reached the bottom of the hill. A huddle of drivers stood across the road outside the bus depot with its grimy bricks and dirt-stained yellow paint; I guess it was near shift change. I bet they had no idea all this stuff was happening on their buses.

"So where, or when, are they from? And why do they do all this helping stuff?"

Eli took a deep breath. "Well, the agency was started by the man who invented time travel. He had a small team who basically just experimented but didn't change anything. Then the daughter of one of the team overdosed on drugs and that got them thinking. They all had kids and had seen, first hand, how hard it was for them and how wrong choices could mess up the rest of their lives, or end them. The team debated the pros and cons, rights and wrongs etc for a long time. In the end, they decided to see whether they could help someone. Afraid they'd mess up the future, they started with just one team of Time Fixers, the son of one of them and the daughter of another. They were both friends of the girl who died and wanted to stop it happening to anyone else."

"Did they go back and help the girl?"

"No, they were tempted, but decided it would be wrong to try and save her because that would cause a paradox."

"A what?"

"Like I said, I don't know much science but I've watched a lot of sci fi and paradoxes are bad. They can, like, end the universe, or something."

"Ugh?"

"Well, the only reason they thought about going to help others was because this girl died but if they went back and stopped that happening then they had no reason to go back."

My face must have looked as blank as my mind because Eli sighed.

"They only decided to go back because she died but if she didn't die, they never would have thought about going back."

I shrugged. "Forget it, that bit's not sticking to any brain cells."

"It skimmed most of mine, as well. Anyway, there was also the chance that the Time Fixers could meet themselves if they went to help someone they already knew. The team didn't like the thought of what chaos that would cause, so they did some research and found a teenager at a nearby school who had died a few years earlier. Her parents had been interviewed by local papers etc so the people from the agency, the Watchers, were able to find out the details about when she first took drugs. They decided to send their son and daughter to some time earlier to make friends with her and try to stop her taking drugs. Before sending them back, they developed a program that looked at events, in history, so they could watch for any changes. That's when they became known as 'The Watchers' because they were watching for people to help and for any changes in time. The son and daughter were 'Time Fixers' because they were trying to help people fix their problems by using Time Travel."

"Did they save her?"

"No, and they didn't save the next two either. They were about to give up but then they succeeded. A boy was being bullied and ran away; his body was found years later. Looks like he'd died of a drug overdose after living rough on the streets for years. The Watchers sent the Fixers back to before he ran. They made friends with him and he stayed home. They kept meeting with him until he'd found some good friends of his own and was fine. Nothing much changed in history so they decided to try and help someone else. It's been going about twenty years now and there are a few teams but not many. The Watchers have to do a lot of research and look at all possible outcomes, and effects on the future, before they even try to help anyone. They've now developed another program that analyses the target's and their family's details and predicts possible effects on their lives if events change. It's amazing really, I've no idea how they do it, but it's been proved right most of the time. They won't help anyone if it would make too big a change, or cause something bad, in the future."

"So how do they choose who to help?"

"It has to be someone whose life is well documented through police reports, court reports or even school notes. If there isn't enough officially recorded, either online or in official archives, there's nothing they can do."

"So, why do they have go-betweens?"

"They do that so that people from our time don't see too much of the future. The son and daughter of the Watchers, you know – the first Time Fixers, became the go-betweens for the first two new teams."

"Does their government know what they're doing?"

"No. They're working in secret because they think the government would use the technology to change the past for their own benefit without thought of how others will be affected. That's another reason they keep it small and it's still run mostly by their families. They research everyone, and their whole lives, before they're invited to join but there's no guarantees. There's always a risk."

"So, they researched me?"

"Yep, and your whole family."

Something inside me twisted, I wasn't sure I wanted someone looking into every bit of my life and future. I especially didn't want them knowing about …

"What's up? You've gone quiet."

I put a stop to my thoughts, nothing good could come of going where my mind always wanted to go.

"So, I guess Emma's case was known because of her death and the police being involved," I said, changing the subject.

"Yes and her father's court case. We travelled back two months to meet Emma so that we'd have chance to go again, if we needed it."

"Only one more chance? There's no way I'll convince her in only one more meeting."

"We'll probably get more but the Watchers limit the amount of contact we have with a target. They don't want to control people's lives. They want to show them there's another way but still leave them to make their own choices. If we go too often it's like we're nagging or manipulating them. Plus, if we're too pushy it might make them react badly and do something that'll make everything worse. It could even have a big impact on the future. We have to be really careful."

"But isn't all this wrong, anyway? I mean, in films where people have gone back and changed the past it's caused all sorts of disasters. There's always some good guy having to stop them. Doesn't that make us the bad guys?"

"No. Like I said, that's fiction." Eli gazed ahead, up the hill, towards the park. His steps slowed while he thought about his answer then picked up again.

"We're not like those in films. We're not out to help ourselves, only others, and if there's any change it'll be the Watchers' time period that's altered, not ours. Our future hasn't happened yet. That's also why they don't help people too far in the past so the impact on their own time isn't as big."

"But they can't be certain."

"No, they can't, but they do a pretty good job of it and they've saved a lot of people."

"Like who?"

"Like Emma."

"No, I mean, who else, specifically?"

He gave me his enigmatic smile and I knew this was one question he wouldn't answer, not yet anyway.

"So why did they pick me? I mean, there must be loads of people better than me."

"I don't know, maybe because you're good at helping others or maybe you want it more and they know you'll do a good job. Is there a reason you'd want it more than anyone else?"

An image flashed into my mind but I pushed it away before tears had chance to form. I shook my head.

"I don't think so," I lied.

Eli shrugged, "Then I don't know, I can ask Zac if you want."

"No, it's okay." I'd pretty much guessed the answer now but I didn't want Eli to know yet. I didn't want to see him wear the sympathetic look that everyone wears when they hear about what happened.

"I can't get my head around all this time stuff."

"Don't worry, I haven't either. I bet there's loads I haven't even thought to ask Zac. Most of the time, I'm interested in the people who need help rather than how they do it."

I decided on a new line of enquiry but one that had rattled around in my brain since I'd first met Eli.

"So, where do you live? Why haven't I seen you around here before and why aren't you ever in uniform?"

"I come from near here but that's all I can say, for now. The rest you'll find out later."

"Why not now?"

"Because it could alter our futures, and my life depends on everything working out the right way, so don't push any more because I'm not going to tell you."

I shook my head. "You're winding me up, aren't you? I mean, your life depends on it and all that, it's a bit melodramatic. This is all a big con, isn't it? I bet Emma's in on it; all this time travel stuff, there's no such thing. That's why you're not telling me about yourself; you don't want me to figure it all out."

Eli smirked, "Really? You think I can make up everything I've just told you? My imagination isn't that good. Anyway, if you think it's not true, explain the disappearing passengers and what happened to your watch."

"I can't, but maybe you chose to talk on the bus to distract me, so I wouldn't notice them getting on and off. And you could have altered my watch when we ducked down and you held my arm."

"Really? Come on, Jess, you know that's not true."

I tried to read his expression, wishing I had a lie detector or something to figure out the truth; this was so 'far fetched', as my gran used to say.

"Okay, if all this is real, how can you be sure the Watchers are working for good? How do you know the story about one of their daughters dying is true?"

Eli fixed his intense gaze on me.

"Because they saved me."

Okay, wasn't expecting that. That's an answer to my 'who specifically have they helped' question.

"How?"

"I can't tell you."

"Aw, come on!"

"Honestly, I can't."

"Why?"

"Because it will affect both our futures."

"That again! How?"

"I can't say, Jess."

"How come you can know and I can't?"

Eli's jaw worked then he sighed. "Because it's in my past but it's in your future."

"Huh?"

Eli held up his hand. "Don't, Jess. I really can't say any more. I might already have said too much."

"But you've just said you're from the future! That's all it can mean if whatever's going to happen is in your past and my future. When are you from?"

"No more, Jess. Really. No more."

Eli's face was set. I wasn't going to get any more answers from him but I couldn't stop the questions burning in my mind.

We reached Rosehill Victoria Park. Grass stretched out in front of us, dotted with trees. A man threw a tennis ball for his dog and the Golden Labrador raced after it, snatched it up and bounded back, only to set off again a few seconds later.

The park made me think of Emma, rocking alone on that swing, her head bowed with sadness and fear.

I shook my head, wishing I could know, for certain, whether this was all a scam or not; but if Emma was in on it, she was a really good actor. I might not be convinced about all the time travel stuff but how could I not go ahead? If I backed out now, and it was real, I would never forgive myself if Emma died because I did nothing. I couldn't face that again …

"Okay, if all this *is* real and I fail, Emma will die."

Whether it was car fumes from the busy road we'd just left, or my fear, I don't know but there was suddenly not enough air.

"She'll die if you don't try," he said, softly. "All we're doing is giving her a chance."

"Have you ever failed a mission?"

Eli's eyes closed. He stuck his hands in his pockets, turned his head away and nodded.

"I'm sorry," I whispered, wishing I hadn't asked.

I wanted to know more but it obviously still bothered him so I couldn't. I knew what it felt like to fail someone; it was the worst feeling ever.

"Let's just try and save Emma," he said, his voice thick with emotion. He strode out across the grass. I jogged to catch up with him.

"Okay," I said. "When do we go?"

"Tomorrow."

***

The next day, I learned nothing, again. If I worked for the agency long my academic career would go down the toilet instead of my head. All the stuff about time travel swam around inside my brain like goldfish in a bowl. It felt so unreal, impossible, but I was buying it because of Emma. She'd looked so sad, like a hurt puppy who just wanted to be loved. I had to see her again and persuade her to get help but how could I ever convince her without telling her everything? It was impossible but if I failed how could I live with myself?

At least, this time, I'd done my homework. With my mobile almost out of data credit, I'd spent lunchtime in the library, online, looking up Childline, the NSPCC and Social Services. I was no expert but at least I knew a bit more about the procedures. I slipped my notes into my bag and left the library, feeling a little more confident.

"Hello, Jess."

I cringed as Lisa sidled up to me. I'd been so busy thinking about Emma, I'd forgotten to keep my 'evil queen' radar on full alert. "I haven't seen you in the café lately. You haven't been avoiding me, have you?"

Actually, yes. Eating sandwiches outside for two days is way better than tangling with you when my mind's already overcrowded with everything else.

That's what I thought but not what I said. Instead, I turned to face her, opened my mouth and words spilled out before my brain engaged.

"Why would anyone want to avoid you, Lisa? You're so sweet and good-natured; you're always kind to everyone and wouldn't hurt a fly."

Lisa's smile made me feel like a mouse about to be swallowed by a snake.

"Oh, Jess, your zip isn't fully fastened." I didn't have time to react as she struck like a snake, whipping out her hand, unzipping my back and snatching my notes, as she spoke. "You need to be careful; you might lose something. Just look at this paper, right near the top." I stared in horror as she held my notes, wafting them in front of me then, within a heartbeat, ripping them to pieces.

"No!" I tried to snatch them back but she was too quick and I watched, helplessly, as she sprinkled them, like confetti, from her hand.

"Oops, sorry, that wasn't important, was it?"

Great, now I'll have to look it all up again, but when?

People walked past, stared and kept going. No one wanted to tangle with Lisa.

"Actually, that was a note from Mrs Freeman, the librarian, for the Head." I lied. "I wonder what to tell him when I see him."

Before I could take a breath, Lisa's hand was on my throat.

"You'll tell him nothing about me, Jess Hardwick, or you'll pay, big time."

She sounded like some small-time gangster but, with her strong grip around my neck, I didn't feel like laughing.

"Okay," I mumbled through my squished windpipe.

Lisa gave me one last glare then let go and sashayed off, her posse close behind. I rubbed my neck.

"Always a pleasure," I muttered.

***

I dressed quickly after Phys. Ed to allow me time to search on my phone and collect those contact numbers again. At least, having found them first on the library pcs, I knew where to look without using too much data. I wrote them down again then entered them into my contacts, as well, to keep them Lisa proof. I pushed the note well down in my bag then headed to history class. I was not going to see Emma unprepared a second time, no matter what Lousy Lisa did to stop me.

***

"I have to go to the ladies," I told Leah, as we left French.

She frowned. "You only live around the corner."

"Yeah, but I've got to fix my makeup."

Leah smiled. "Are you meeting that boy again?"

I wanted to deny it, to avoid embarrassment, but there was no point, she'd find out for herself as soon as we got outside.

"Yeah, but that's not why I'm doing my makeup."

"Oh yeah, so why are you doing it?" Leah followed me into the ladies and stood by the door watching me apply foundation in front of the mirror.

Okay, Jess, dig yourself out of this one.

What could I say? I couldn't tell her the truth that I was covering up my bruises so that it looked as though time had passed. "Er, I just am."

That was so pathetic.

"You're making yourself look good for him!" Leah left the door and walked over to stand beside me, watching me through the mirror, as I applied another layer to the darker bruises. "So, who is he then?"

I shrugged. "A guy I met."

"Where?"

"Outside school."

"How come?"

"Ugh?"

"How come you met him outside school? I've not seen him around before. He's not from here, is he?"

"No."

"So why was he here if he goes to another school?" Her eyes widened. "Has he been expelled?"

"No!" This was getting out of hand. "No, look, he was just here to meet someone and he saw me and, well, that was it really."

"You mean, love at first sight? That's so romantic."

"No! Not love, we're just friends, is all."

"You don't freshen up your makeup for 'just friends' especially when that friend is a boy and hot."

Heat rose up from my neck and into my cheeks. The problem was, I did fancy Eli; who wouldn't? But I didn't want to, I mean, just three days ago he'd watched me being beaten up. He might have told me the reason for that but it still left a twisted feeling in my stomach. How could I care for a guy who stood by and watched me getting battered, for whatever reason? And all this Time Agency stuff had yet to be proven. He could still be some kind of weirdo who just happened to know Emma. Although, as he's trying to help her, I guess he's a good weirdo but still, not my boyfriend and I didn't need the complication of everyone thinking he was.

"Look, he's not my boyfriend. Okay?" I grimaced at the harshness in my voice.

Leah looked wounded. "Okay, sorry." Her head dropped and she fingered the sink. "I didn't mean to upset you."

Way to go, Jess. Snap at the friend least able to take it.

"Don't worry about it, you didn't upset me. Will you do my eye shadow? I'm useless at it."

Leah's head came up and her face brightened. "Okay."

Five minutes later we walked across the car park. Chad, Dwaine, Jake, Tammy and Queenie stood waiting beside the gates.

Leah's lips were squashed beneath Jake's fangs as soon as she was in reach. Turning away, so I didn't lose my lunch, I spotted Eli leaning in his usual position. My stomach immediately did a back flip. Was that a result of seeing Eli or the fear of failing Emma? I wish I knew.

"See you tomorrow guys!" I called and set off towards him.

"That's her new boyfriend." I heard Leah tell the others. "But she doesn't want us to know about him yet."

"Looks like a chav," Jake scoffed.

"Jake!" Leah hissed. "No, he doesn't."

"Yeah, he really does. Hey, Chav!"

I cringed but Eli simply pushed himself off the railings and looked at me as I drew level with him.

"Sorry about Jake, he's a jerk."

"Yeah, I figured that one out," Eli said and turned towards Blythe Avenue.

"A coward as well!" Jake's taunts followed us.

"Jake!" Leah cried.

The sooner she broke up with that idiot, the better.

Thankfully, we heard nothing more as we walked towards the corner and the usual bus stop.

"Are you ready for this?" Eli asked when we finally settled into our seats, mid-way down the bus.

"My stomach doesn't know what it's doing," I said, "But I think it might be the Salsa."

Eli grinned, his lopsided grin. "Yeah, I know what that feels like. Look, just take it as it comes, okay? Don't push too hard. You can only try your best. You can't make it any worse than it would've been without us. When we get there, it's just over two weeks since you last saw her. She's now in February.

You can tell her they've found your mum and you're going to move in with her. That will explain why she hasn't seen you at school. You can say you're still going to your old school. Okay?"

I nodded. My throat closed up tight.

"Duck." Eli's breath brushed my ear, causing shivers down my neck and into my spine, as we slid down in our seats, his hand on mine.

A warm glow emanating from his touch made me want to stay slouched in that seat forever.

Give over, Jess. I silently commanded. *You do NOT fancy him.*

"Jess." I turned to look at him, the glow reaching my heart. "We can sit up now."

"Oh." I hadn't noticed the dizzy feeling come and go. Maybe that was just my confusion on the last trip, and nothing to do with time travel, or was I just too distracted by the sensations Eli's touch caused in my body?

I sat up quickly and looked out of the window, chewing my thumb.

"Is everything okay?"

"Yeah, I'm fine," I lied. I'd never felt like this about a boy before. Why did it have to be someone like Eli? And with all this other stuff going on, at the same time, my head could seriously explode.

As we stepped off the bus, and stood opposite the same park, a whole troupe of girls danced in my stomach.

"She should be in the same place."

"How do you know where she'll be each day; that can't be documented, can it?"

"It's from witness statements. In fine weather she always sits in the park. In bad weather she hangs around school for a while before setting off home."

"Oh."

Pushing the doubts from my mind, I crossed the road and paused as I entered the park.

Come on, Jess. You can do this.

Taking a deep breath, I walked towards the children's play area, opened the gate and dropped onto the same swing as last time.

"Hi," I said, watching Emma gently rock beside me.

"Hi," she said, her eyes focussed on the ground.

"Are you okay?"

She nodded. "I'm Emma, by the way, I never told you before."

I bit my tongue, just managing not to say, 'I know'.

"I'm Jess."

"Yes, you told me before."

She looked up and I gasped, a fresh bruise darkened her left eye.

"Oh, Emma." I reached out but stopped short of touching it, I didn't want to hurt her. "When did that happen?"

"Yesterday; I burnt Dad's dinner," she murmured, looking back down at her feet. "It was my fault."

"No, Emma, it wasn't. Everyone makes mistakes but no one deserves to be hit for them."

"But he's tired when he comes in from work; he needs a decent meal."

"Are those your words, or his?"

She didn't answer, she just rocked backwards and forwards, the old iron swing creaking.

"I used to think it was my fault too," I lied. Or maybe it wasn't a lie. I always blamed myself for being big-mouthed or stubborn when Lisa bullied me. I guess if someone tells you it's your fault often enough you start to believe it. "Even though I messed up sometimes, he shouldn't have hit me and your dad shouldn't either. Emma, haven't your teachers noticed your bruises?"

She nodded. "But I told them I'm getting bullied. They asked me who it is but I said I'd deal with it. It's only the second time it's showed; usually dad hits me where it won't be seen."

At that moment, I wanted to hit her dad where it wouldn't be seen, preferably in a very tender part of his anatomy.

Emma's swing stopped.

"Is it really okay in foster care?" Her voice was so quiet I hardly heard her.

"Yes," I said, quickly, then realised I'd been too eager. "Well, it's not the same as living in your own house but it's safer."

"You weren't in school," she said, "I looked for you."

"No, erm, they've decided there's no point. They found my mum."

Emma's head shot up.

"That was quick."

"Yeah, turns out she was using her maiden name and had only moved once since leaving dad, so they found her pretty quickly. She came to see me last week. I'm going to live with her."

"She wants you?"

"Yeah." I tried to remember all that Eli had said about Emma's mum. "It turns out Dad was hitting her too. She was scared so she left. She didn't have anywhere to go and never thought Dad would hurt me, so she left me behind. She was real upset when she found out what's been going on."

Emma's eyes moistened. "What was it like, meeting her?"

I swallowed. It was hard to imagine seeing my mum for the first time in years when I actually see her every day.

"Well, it was awkward at first, you know, a bit like strangers but we got talking and, after a while, it was like she'd never left. It was great."

Emma's face brightened, just a little.

"My mum left because Dad used to hit her. I think she loved me though."

"Oh, she did!" I clamped my mouth shut, suddenly realising I wasn't supposed to know that. "Well, mine did," I added, quickly, "And I'm sure your mum did too."

"Was it worth it?" Emma's head tilted to one side, her hands tightly gripping the chains. "You know, reporting your dad and everything?"

"Yes, it was." I paused, trying to find the right words. "It was scary but definitely worth it. I'm going to live with my mum and Dad can't hurt me any more."

Emma sat for ages, just looking at me and rocking gently, while my stomach churned. Had I said enough? Had I said too much? Should I speak or let her think?

"What did you do?" she asked, eventually.

"What, me and Mum?"

"No, how did you get help?"

"Oh. I called Childline."

"What was it like?"

"Real scary, at first, but okay."

My heart was beating so fast it's a wonder Emma couldn't hear it. I felt so close to saving her, I couldn't ruin it now.

"Do you want to call them? You don't have to tell them who you are, if you don't want to, you can just talk to them."

"Really?"

"Yes."

Emma sat totally still, staring out across the park.

"I don't have to tell them anything?"

"No, not if you don't want to."

"Have you got their number?"

"Yes, it's here." I fished the piece of paper from my bag; glad I'd looked up the number again. "Do you want to ring them now?"

Emma shook her head. "No, I'll do it later. I've got to think about it some more."

"Are you sure? I'll stay with you while you ring, if you like?"

What if she didn't ring and the Watchers didn't let me come back because of their 'no nagging' rule?

"No thanks, Jess, but you've helped me a lot." She shoved the paper into her coat pocket. "It's been good to talk to someone who understands. I've never told anyone before."

I just managed to stop myself before blurting out 'I know'.

"You will think about it?"

Emma nodded.

"Okay," I said, not able to stop my heart from dropping like a deflated balloon. I wanted to push, to insist she ring straight away but knew I couldn't. If I was too insistent, I'd frighten her off. If only she knew what was at stake, and how urgent it was, she'd definitely ring; it seemed stupid not to be able to tell her.

"Emma," I began without thinking.

"I've got to go now." She stood abruptly and picked up her bag.

"Yes, but Emma…"

She glanced at her watch. "I've really got to go. Thanks for talking to me."

I felt like grabbing her arm and not letting her go until she made that call but instead I watched her walk slowly out of the park and hoped I'd done enough.

"There's other numbers on the paper that might help too!" I called, just before she disappeared from view.

A couple of minutes later, Eli sauntered into sight. My heart beat faster at the sight of him.

Behave yourself. I silently commanded. *Only Emma matters right now.*

"How'd it go?" he asked, sinking onto Emma's swing.

"I don't know. She listened and seemed interested but wouldn't make the call." I remembered the longing in Emma's face when she thought about living with her mum and wished I could make it all work out for her. "Why can't we tell her the truth?"

"She'd never believe you."

"Couldn't the Watchers take her forward in time and let her see what will happen? Then she'd believe."

"But she can't know her own future, no one can."

"Why not, if it will save her life?"

"Because that's how life is. We all make decisions that affect our futures without knowing how it'll turn out. All we can do is try to make the right ones. Our job is to point Emma in the right direction and let her know she has a choice."

"But I don't want her to die!"

I could feel her slipping away, just like …

"I know." Eli seemed so calm I felt like slapping him. "I don't either."

I stood and paced across the grass.

"How can you be so calm? If she dies it'll be our fault."

"No, it'll be her father's fault."

Eli stepped up, took hold of my shoulders and stopped me pacing.

"Jess, you're doing your best, that's all anyone can ever do. We're not here to manipulate people, like puppets. We let them know there's an alternative; we try to help them to help themselves and that's it. Ultimately the choice is theirs and that's how it has to be."

"But why?"

Eli shrugged. "Because we all have our own lives to live, I guess. We have to make our own decisions and take the consequences."

"Her teachers saw the bruises, she told them she was being bullied but why didn't they call Social Services, just in case?"

"Zac says it all came out later in the investigation and court case. The teachers only noticed her bruises in her last couple of months and they accepted her explanations about bullying. I guess her dad must have been getting worse. It's the teachers' observations that told us the best time to visit, when the sight of the bruises would open up the conversation for you. By the time the teachers realised her excuses were lies, and reported the suspected abuse, it was too late."

I sighed, poor Emma, if only she'd spoken up.

"When do we find out what happens?"

"Tomorrow."

"Can't we find out today? Like now? Don't the Watchers know already? I mean, they're in the future, aren't they?"

"Yes, but I'm not telepathic. I have to wait for them to tell Zac and for him to tell me."

Another wait. Don't the Watchers know I'm not a patient person? Obviously not, or they'd have picked someone else for the job.

***

The next twenty-four hours were a nightmare; I didn't sleep, again, and learned ziltch in school. The teachers gave me stern looks and my friends kept nudging each other and whispering, convinced love was the reason. I wished it was that simple.

Hoping to avoid Lisa, I ate sandwiches outside again at lunch. Thankfully, it was pretty warm for March, so at least I didn't get frost bite. Mixed teams thwacked tennis balls over the nets on the courts below me.

As I finished my apple, a shadow fell across my legs.

"Here you are, young Jess." My insides turned to mush at the sound of Lisa's voice. "So this is where you've been hiding."

"Yeah sure, I'm hiding. That's why I'm sitting here in plain sight," I lied.

Lisa grinned. "Sure, whatever you say. I always knew you were pigheaded but I never knew you were a coward. Guess everyone can be wrong sometimes, even me. Come on, girls." With a flick of her long, blonde hair she led her posse down towards the tennis courts. I guessed they were on the lookout for talent but I pitied any lads who got ensnared by those four; it'd be like dating praying mantises.

"What did Lisa want?" Tammy asked, dropping down beside me.

"Just to call me a coward for not eating in the café; she thinks I'm hiding from her."

"Well, you are, aren't you?"

"Yeah, but that doesn't make me a coward, it just makes me sensible. I'm avoiding trouble."

"That's new for you." Queenie lowered herself down on the other side of me. "Maybe this new boyfriend of yours is teaching you some sense."

"He's not my boyfriend."

"Yeah, sure," Tammy said. "And you're glazed over in lessons because you're planning how to save the world."

"Something like that."

They gave each other knowing looks and grinned.

"So, where's Leah?" I asked, hoping to change the subject.

"Oh, Jake whisked her off for a necking session behind the sports hall," Queenie answered.

"Okay, so that makes me feel sick," Tammy said, with a grimace.

"I wish she'd pack him in." I shuddered at the thought of Jake slobbering all over her.

"Yeah, well, that's not gonna happen any time soon." Queenie plucked at the grass and sprinkled loose blades over her shoes. "He's her first boyfriend and she's infatuated and, even if she wasn't, she'd never have the guts to end it."

I knew Queenie was right and it made me even more worried about her. I could feel another serious advice session brewing.

As soon as all the business with Emma was sorted and my head was straight again, I'd focus on

Leah. Separating her from Jake would be my next mission.

***

At the end of the day, I rushed out, not even bothering to wait for my friends.

Eli was in his usual spot but, instead of casually leaning, he stood watching the school entrance. Was that a good sign or bad? Part of me wanted to race to him and hear the news and another part wanted to run the other way and never find out.

I forced myself to walk calmly towards him.

"What happened?" I asked, my voice barely audible over passing cars and the voices of everyone chatting as they walked home.

Eli slowly shook his head.

"She doesn't make the call," he said, his voice soft. "I'm sorry, Jess, but Emma still dies."

***

CHAPTER FIVE – LAST CHANCE

I gasped, feeling like a hammer had just slammed into my chest. I'd failed. An image of Emma, her eyes wide and hopeful, filled my mind.

"But she said she'd ring! Why didn't she?"

"She only said she'd think about it. Either she decided not to or she just said that to make you feel better." Eli shrugged. "Either way, it doesn't happen."

"How can you be so calm, again? A girl's life was in our hands and we failed."

"I know and I'm not calm. Just because I don't rant like you doesn't mean I don't care."

"I don't rant!" I growled. "Why wasn't I given training? Why wasn't I told what to say? Those future people must know what's needed. Why did they just leave me to muddle it; especially when it's my first assignment?"

A couple of year seven boys stared as they walked past. I glared back at them.

"They don't know everything, Jess. They can't read people's minds or know what will reach a person and what won't; that's why they pick Time Fixers who are about the same age, from around the same time period and local. That way, they give us the best chance of knowing what to say. They give us an idea of how to reach the person but that's all they can do."

"But they're in the future so they should know how it turns out and you said they have a machine that gives them possible outcomes or timelines or something."

"They know the future as it stands. Their computer system can suggest possible outcomes if major events are effected; for example, whether a person lives instead of dies, but they can't say how every word or small action will effect anything, who could? The Watchers are human beings, not God. There's no way of knowing how to reach someone, we can only do our best. As a girl you knew how to reach her better than me. She probably wouldn't have talked to me at all."

I huffed, not very lady-like but I felt close to exploding. "You said you care but you've a funny way of showing it, just standing there blaming me."

"I'm not blaming you. I only meant you were the best person for the job. You're a girl, the same age and you know what it's like being beaten up. Like I said before, her dad's to blame, not us. And what do you want me to do? Would it change anything if I paced around wringing my hands?"

"It might." I knew he was right but I wanted to lash out at someone and he was the nearest person. Actually, he was the only person I could even talk to about this.

"Isn't there anything else we can do?"

"Yes, if you're willing to go on." Eli's gaze was intense.

I felt transfixed by those eyes, almost hypnotised, saying no was impossible but I didn't want to anyway.

"Of course, I'm willing."

"Let's talk." He turned and took his usual route towards Blythe Avenue.

"Are we going now?"

"No, we can't today. We have to wait. I know you covered your bruises up last time to make it look like two weeks had passed for you, as well as for Emma. But this time we will be going to the day she dies. Your bruises have to be invisible."

"Why are we waiting so long? What if I need more than one more chance at this?"

"It's like I said. Emma has to make up her own mind; you can't nag her into it. The Watchers want to help people but they don't want to take over their lives. They've decided we can go again a week on Wednesday."

"But the last day? Eli, what if I fail?"

"Don't."

"But what if I do?"

"Then history will stay the same."

"You mean, she'll die."

"Yes." Eli said, softly. "But if she decides she wants help but can't get it for herself, for any reason, we can wade in and get her out."

"How are we supposed to know she definitely wants help? Like the Watchers, we're not mind readers and anyway, we can travel in time, if it goes wrong, we could just try again, couldn't we?" I felt like a kid being asked to fly a rocket to the moon. I mean, advising my friends was one thing but having a girl's life in my hands was something else.

"I'll decide whether we intervene or not, depending on what happens, but if I'm not sure we'll have to leave and wait for the Watchers to get back to us. Physical intervention is dangerous and can cause time contaminations."

"What?"

"It can wreck the future for a lot of people."

"How?"

"For example, if I intervene in the past and am, say, killed or seriously hurt; what happens if people witness it or the police or hospitals are involved? My parents, in the past, would be informed of my death. They would see my 'older' body or visit me in hospital then the 'me' from their own time arrives home from school. Can you imagine their shock? How would anyone explain it? And what about me? At best, my parents would never let me out of their sight. At worst, I'd become a lab rat while the authorities try to figure it out; but even worse than that, all the people I've helped would never be helped.'

'Even if that doesn't happen, if we keep going back, we could end up meeting ourselves from our last visit or people could see two of us; the more we go back the more likely this will happen. Because of that, we can't go to the same moment and just redo it. Zac says it would cause a paradox."

"Oh yeah, you said those are bad, right?"

"Right."

Can I have, like, ten years to get my neurons around all this? Talk about complicated. I don't even watch sci-fi. The future in my hands; who on earth (or in the future) thought I was actually up to this?

My brain felt totally fried so I let it wonder off on a tangent and ask a question that had niggled me since Leah first saw Eli.

"What school do you go to?"

Eli stuck his hands in his pockets and kept walking, looking straight ahead.

"And how can you be outside my school as soon as the bell rings?"

Eli still didn't answer.

"You've been expelled, haven't you? Is that because of the agency, missing too much time or not concentrating on your lessons?" I thought of the look on my teachers' faces these last few days. "Am I gonna end up expelled, as well?"

A smile crept across his lips.

"No, I haven't been expelled. I work for a *time* agency, Jess. They can arrange for me to be outside your school whenever they want me there."

"But you said you're local, so which school? And I know you're from the future, so how far?"

"You've asked before, Jess, and like I said last time, you'll find out later. There's no point keeping asking the same question in a different way."

"I haven't asked about your school before and, anyway, you might have slipped up and told me."

"Nice try."

"You said my knowing could alter both our futures, but why?"

Eli shook his head. "Leave it, Jess."

I tried a bit longer but got no more out of him. Sometimes Eli was so frustrating. How could he tell me so much and yet leave me with more questions than when he began?

***

Waiting for that Wednesday was almost impossible. My friends decided I was totally in love because my mind wandered so much. My teachers scowled at me and I knew a serious discussion about my 'academic career' was on the horizon. I just hoped we'd save Emma soon for her sake and so that I could get back to my usual, not-quite-brainy self before the teachers went off on one. I still ate outside to avoid Lisa. If this went on much longer I'd end up a real 'Billy-no-mates' not to mention having pneumonia; the warm days had deserted me and we were back to freezing March, with a vengeance! But with everything running through my head, I couldn't deal with Lisa as well.

***

As soon as the week-and-a-half passed I wished it hadn't. All that waiting; what if it was for nothing? What if I failed? I ran my tongue around the inside of my mouth; sore from constant chewing. I was gonna end up a nervous wreck, at this rate.

Even the sight of Eli, casually leaning against the railings in a blue hoodie, didn't settle the acrobatics in my stomach, in fact, they got worse.

"Are you ready?" he asked, gazing down at me.

I nodded. Speech was out of the question.

We walked to the bus stop, climbed onboard and sat near the back. I watched gardens filled with half-grown and budding daffodils zip past the windows.

"Duck," Eli hissed. I ducked, feeling the now familiar dizziness, and when Eli gave the 'all clear' I sat up to rain-streaked windows. Bright yellow daffodils bent under the heavy downpour and strong winds.

"What?"

Eli grinned. He stared out for a couple of minutes then explained. "It's Thursday in the second week of April; the Easter holidays start at the weekend."

"We've gone into the future?" I whispered.

"By nearly two weeks."

I turned to him, stunned.

"Wow." Was all I could manage.

"Yeah, wow. It never gets old." His eyes glistened.

I grinned. "Time travel is amazing!"

"Yep! And we're here."

Eli stood and walked to the front of the bus. I pulled myself up, my legs wobbly as our mission sprang back into mind.

"So, are we going to the park again?" I asked, stepping down onto the curb.

Eli shook his head, rain already soaking his hair and running down into his eyes. I was only wearing a thin jacket and, although I pulled up the collar, it was only a matter of minutes before it was soaked through. I wanted to have a rant about the Watchers not warning us to wear monsoon resistant clothing but my stomach was too busy doing an impression of a washing machine on spin cycle.

"Emma's late coming home because of the rain; she'll be coming around the corner in about one minute."

"I know the Watchers found out about her staying late at school when it rains but there's no way they can know exactly where she is at any time on a specific day!"

"This isn't just any day, Jess. This is the day she dies; there are witness statements, CCTV footage etc. You've seen reconstructions on TV? Well, they pieced together everything that happened after school up to the point she died. It was all presented at her dad's trial."

My heart lodged so tightly in my throat, as I stared at the corner, I felt it might choke me.

"What should I say?"

When there was no answer, I turned and couldn't believe it. Eli had gone. How could he keep leaving me to work everything out for myself? That boy was so infuriating!

I made a quick decision and started walking towards the corner. Our meeting had to look casual, not rehearsed. I snorted inside.

Rehearsed, fat chance. Fighters got more warning of a knockout.

I was about six metres from the corner when a trainer appeared followed by the rest of Emma. She walked with slow steps and bowed head as though life was too heavy for her; I guess it was.

"Hi!" I said, trying to sound surprised.

Emma looked up and her eyes widened in recognition. "Oh, hi! I haven't seen you in ages! Are you okay?"

"Yeah, I'm great. How about you?"

Her head dropped again.

"Okay."

"You don't look okay."

Emma scuffed her feet on the wet ground and stayed silent. Rain pounded around us, hitting so hard the drops splattered, sending spray up over our toes.

"I'm not so great, I guess," she said, eventually.

"You want to talk about it?"

"It wouldn't do any good."

"It might."

"Won't you be cold?"

She looked at my inadequate jacket that was dripping so fast it looked like I was wearing my own personal rain cloud.

"I'll be okay," I said, with an involuntary shiver. Rain trickled down my back and my trousers clung to my legs like a wetsuit. "I was running late and grabbed the first thing I could find when I set off for school this morning. I haven't been home yet, I'm on my way to a friend's. It isn't far."

"Oh. Who's your friend? I might know them."

Heck. I've dropped myself in it again.

"Oh, er, well, er, you might not she, er, goes to a private school but I met her when I stayed around here in foster care."

Okay, I'm a terrible liar – so sue me!

"Oh. Well, don't let me hold you up."

Emma stepped out to go around me but I stepped in her path.

"It's okay. She'll not mind if I'm a bit late; she's not much of a time keeper."

"But you'll be soaked."

I grinned through the river running down my face. "I'm already soaked and so are you, a bit more won't hurt." Wind drove the rain against my back and into Emma's face. Even having her hood up wasn't doing her much good. "I'll tell you what. Why don't we talk under there?"

I pointed across the road towards a shop with an awning outside. No one was around, because of the rain, so our conversation would still be private.

"Ok-ay." She chewed her lip.

"Don't you want to talk?"

"Yes! Yes, I want to." She paused. "Because you know how it feels. It's just that ... I'm not used to talking about it, you know, and I don't want to put you out."

I smiled. "You're not putting me out."

We checked traffic and crossed over the road. Finally out of the rain, I waited for Emma to begin but she didn't. She glanced around; her hands pushed firmly into her pockets. I watched her, not sure whether to ask questions or leave her to talk in her own time.

"What was it like with your dad?" she asked, eventually.

I swallowed. What could I say?

"Well, he, er, he was okay most of the time but he, like, had a short fuse, you know? If something didn't go right he took it out on me."

"My dad's like that. He's a good dad though; he makes sure I'm looked after."

Yeah, right, with his fist.

"He doesn't mean to hurt me; he loves me."

She started out hesitantly, chewing her thumb, but before long it all poured out. She was like a coke bottle that'd been shaken too long. Now she'd taken the top off everything came gushing out. Constantly looking around to make sure we weren't overheard, she told me that at first her dad was only violent when drunk but lately he didn't have to be drunk. He was angry all the time and, no matter how hard she tried to please him, he always found something wrong. She said that when he hit her he always turned the music up loud so no one would hear her cries.

"I'm so scared of loud music." Her voice sounded croaky and broken, like she had a mega cold. She wiped tears away then gnawed on her thumb again.

I didn't speak until her words finally ran out.

"Emma, do you want me to help you get away from him?"

She looked at me, her whole face radiating longing, and nodded.

"Yes," she whispered. "I thought about ringing that number you gave me but I love my dad and couldn't do it. I don't want to get him into trouble. I *still* love him but I don't think I want to live with him anymore. If I ask for help, will he get in trouble?"

Her eyes were like deep pools filled with sadness.

"He might," I said, wishing I could say something else. "But what he's doing is wrong. If you stay, he'll just keep hitting you and it could get worse."

It will get worse, I wanted to shout. *Loads worse. You have to leave now!*

"If you leave now, hopefully the authorities will help your dad get counselling, or something. If they help him with his temper his life will be better."

Emma stood, her eyes fixed somewhere in the distance, while she thought it over.

"Do you want to ring them now?" I asked, eventually. "You can use my mobile."

Emma frowned but nodded.

Feeling my heart pound with hope, I pulled my mobile from my bag, dialled 0800 1111 and waited for it to ring.

"Here you go." I held it out to Emma. She started to reach for it then pulled back.

"I daren't."

"Go on, it's okay. I did it," I lied.

"What shall I say?"

"Tell them everything."

Emma shook her head and backed off, a speck of blood appearing on the end of her thumb.

"I can't."

Hearing a voice answer, "You're through to someone you can talk to." I quickly pressed the 'end call' button.

"Why not?" I asked, squeezing the phone tight in my hand.

"What if Dad finds out before they get me out of there? He'll be real mad."

Her eyes were huge and scared, like a puppy's.

"Look, I can't promise anything but it's better to at least talk to them. You don't have to tell them who you are until you want to.

Please call them, I urged, silently.

Emma chewed again, not noticing the cut or the drop of blood that had dripped onto her bottom lip. She caught sight of my watch, just visible at the end of my soggy jacket sleeve, and her head snapped up. "It's five o'clock! Dad'll be home in half-an-hour; if his dinner isn't ready he'll kill me!"

My heart wrenched at her words.

She quickly dug into her school bag and handed me her maths book.

"I threw away the number in case Dad found it. Write it in there," she said, "Dad never looks in it; he hates maths."

As soon as I'd finished writing, she snatched the book back and stuffed it into the bottom of her bag.

"You will call?" I asked, as she rushed away.

She stopped for a moment and our eyes met.

"Are you happy with your mum?"

"Yeah, real happy," I said, truthfully.

She smiled. "I'll tell Dad I'm going to a friend's to do homework after tea and ring then. I won't tell them who I am, to start with, and see how it goes. But if they sound okay I'll tell them, so I can leave. And I'll ask them to look after my dad and get him help. I want him to be happy."

With a final wave she rushed away into the rain.

I watched her go, not sure whether to be hopeful or devastated. Had I failed again or would she actually make the call?

Once she was out of sight, Eli emerged from behind a garden wall about six houses away. He was so wet he looked as though he'd been swimming fully dressed.

"How did it go?" he asked, joining me under the awning.

I couldn't answer. I stared at the corner, where Emma had disappeared, feeling like I'd just watched someone jump off a cliff.

Turning to Eli, I found him examining my face.
"You don't think she'll ring, do you?"
"I don't know," I croaked, "She wants to but she's scared he'll find out and hurt her, and at the same time she loves him and wants to protect him."

Eli shook his head. "Unbelievable," he muttered.

I thought for a minute. "I'm not sure. I mean, he's her dad, isn't he? He's all she's got. She says she'll make up an excuse to get out and ring but what if it isn't soon enough? What time is she killed?"

Eli stuck his hands in his pockets and shook his head.

"I don't know, I didn't ask." He frowned. "I should have asked. I guess all we can do now is wait."

***

On the bus home we sat up after the time shift and received some pretty curious looks. We were totally drenched on what was, in our own time, a dry day.

I couldn't begin to dream up a believable excuse for Mum. 'Someone's sprinkler came on just as I passed their garden.' 'I fell down a manhole.' 'A water-main burst, a car drove through it and sprayed water all over me.' None of them explained why I looked as though I'd been thrown in a lake. It's a pity there isn't a river on the way home; I could say I'd fallen in.

I peered through our living-room window while droplets of water fell from my trousers and formed a puddle at my feet. Mum stood ironing in front of the TV. Could I sneak in without her hearing me? I turned the handle slowly, tiptoed into the hall and peeped around the living-room door, to make sure Mum wasn't looking, before dodging past and upstairs. Thankfully, Abby was at drama class and Jimmy's door was closed so I dashed into my room, grabbed some clean clothes and nipped into the bathroom.

After a hot shower, I finally stopped shivering.

***

Sleep escaped me that night so the next morning I felt grotty and grimaced at my white face in the bathroom mirror. Bloodshot eyes, underlined with black circles and edged with the final remnants of yellow-brown bruises, made me look like an accident victim.

I needed an almost professional make-up job to make me look anywhere near decent.

Abby was so loud at breakfast, I wished she had a volume control; for a small kid she could make megaphones redundant.

Every step towards school was an effort until I turned the last corner and stopped dead, like I'd hit an invisible wall.

Eli stood in his usual spot but he was edgy, stepping from foot to foot. As soon as he saw me, he started towards me.

"We've got to go," he said.

"I can't, I've got school!"

"It can't be helped; we have to go now. If all goes well, they'll bring us back to more or less the same time."

"What do you mean, 'if all goes well', how could it go wrong?"

"Lots of ways; one of us could be hurt. We can't predict what'll happen and whether we'll be able to catch the right bus."

"What happens if we don't?"

"We have to wait until the Watchers realise we missed the pick-up-point and send Zac to tell us another bus to catch."

"How long will that take?"

"I don't know."

"But they will get us back to our own time?"

"Should do. I've never had to find out. Look, that part should be okay but this isn't an easy mission."

"It's never easy."

"Okay, so it's harder, more dangerous then."

"Why?"

"Jess, Emma still dies but the Watchers agree she wanted help so they've decided we can intervene. Emma tells her father she needs to do homework at a friend's house – just like she told you she would but, because of a problem with the meal, her father gets angry and that's when it happens."

"How do they know this?"

"They've seen the transcripts from her father's trial."

"Oh, yeah, forgot about that."

"We're going to the house, just before it happens, that's why it's dangerous. Are you willing to risk it?"

My stomach somersaulted. "Are you?"

Eli's mouth was a thin line but he nodded.

"Me too then."

"You sure?"

I nodded, how could I not? Emma needed us.

"Come on," Eli turned and strode towards the bus stop. I had to jog to keep up, my school bag bouncing against my back.

"Jess, where're you going?" Queenie called, behind me.

I half-turned, still following Eli, "It's okay, I'll be back!"

Great, now I sound like Arnold Schwarzenegger in 'The Terminator'.

I pushed it from my mind and hurried after Eli.

"But, why are we rushing? It's time travel; we can go any time, can't we?"

"We could but, because the incident happens only a couple of hours after you last spoke to her, they want you back as soon as possible so you'll remember everything that was said. It's already been overnight for you; they don't want it stretching any longer. She'll expect it to be as fresh for you as it is for her; if you sound hesitant about anything either of you said, or if you get something wrong, she could distrust you and die because of it."

"But I can remember everything."

"Maybe now but will you still remember after a day at school when your mind's been filled with algebra, history and lit? We can't afford any mistakes."

"Don't they think I can do this?" I asked as we reached the bus stop.

"Of course they do or we wouldn't be going back. Look, they've got loads of experience; they don't directly intervene very often but, when they do, they've found that if we're returning to a time shortly after the last contact with the target then it's best to go back asap."

"I'd rather have time to plan."

"Plan what? We're going into the house, if we can, and we don't know what will be happening. We can have a basic plan but that's all, mostly we'll be winging it."

"But, if it goes wrong, we can go back and try again, can't we?"

"And meet ourselves or have Emma and her dad see two of us? Like I said before, we can't keep going back to exactly the same time to try over and over."

Okay, I get it.

The bus arrived and we climbed onboard, discussion over.

We rode in silence. I don't know about Eli but the enormity of what we were about to do occupied every millimetre of my consciousness. As usual, we ducked when Eli indicated and when he stood to press the stop button I felt as though I was heading for the dentist's chair.

We were back on the same day when I'd met Emma in the rain. Thankfully, the rain had stopped but the air was still cool and puddles covered the ground. It was later in the evening and, with heavy rain clouds still hovering, it seemed more like midnight.

"So, we're going to knock and try to see Emma. We've got to get her to come with us," Eli explained as we walked down a long, straight road.

"What if she won't come? Or, what if her dad answers and won't let us see her?"

"If she won't come then there's nothing we can do, she's made her choice, but if she wants to come and her dad won't let her then that's when we wing it. Follow my lead. No matter what happens, you get Emma out. Forget about me and go."

"What do you mean, 'forget about you and go'? What are you going to be doing?"

"Anything I have to."

I didn't like the sound of that, my palms were hot and sweaty, despite the cold, and every nerve prickled. Taking slow, deep breaths, I tried to calm myself but it didn't work.

Eli stopped outside a semi-detached house with a neatly cut lawn, bordered by white daffodils and bright pansies. The double-glazed windows and doors were spotlessly clean.

"Is this it?" I asked, amazed that anything bad could happen inside this perfect house.

"Yeah." A small frown creased Eli's forehead while his jaw worked and his hands clenched and unclenched. I shivered. Until then, Eli had always seemed so confident but seeing him look as nervous as me brought home how easily this could all go wrong.

"Have you ever done anything like this before?" I asked, willing him to say 'yes'.

Eli shook his head and I gulped on the tennis ball in my throat.

"Every job is different. We have to do what's needed."

Breathe, I told myself, *Just breathe.*

"Are you ready?" Eli looked down at me, his face pale.

My head nodded but my heart cried 'No!' Right then, a dunking from Lisa didn't seem too bad. I almost wished I could choose that instead of this. Only the thought of Emma's sad face kept me going.

"Okay, let's go." Eli opened the small, iron side-gate and strode up the drive. I followed, trying to hide behind him. After all my brave talk at school, if Lisa and co. could see me now they'd know the truth, it's all an act; I'm not brave at all.

"Okay," Eli said, his voice determined. "First we knock. Hopefully, her dad's 'respectable image' will stop him doing anything with witnesses around but remember, whatever happens, it's your job to get Emma out of the house."

We reached the door and immediately it was obvious plan 'A' wasn't going to work. Loud music boomed from inside. My whole body turned cold, Emma was afraid of loud music because that's when her father hits her.

I could tell by Eli's frantic hammering that he'd realised the significance as well. Music boomed on and no one came to the door. Eli took a deep breath.

"Okay, we're going in."

***

CHAPTER SIX - RESCUE

My heart beat in time with the base drum as Eli turned the handle. Thankfully, the door opened and we stepped into a long, off-white hall with a door on our left followed by carpeted stairs. There was another door on our right and a third at the far end of the hall. Eli peered into the room on our left. I followed and saw an oak desk, a wooden filing cabinet and a large, black leather chair. The whole room was dark with horrible brown wallpaper.

I crossed to the room on the right, on legs that felt so weak I was amazed they were still holding me up. The lounge had cream wallpaper, carpet and suite and a huge TV hanging on the opposite wall but no people.

Our checks had taken just seconds and now there was only one more room to explore on the ground floor. It was the source of the booming music and as we approached we heard Emma plead.

"No, Dad, please! I'm sorry."

A glance passed between us then we ran. I entered the kitchen just after Eli and took in Emma cowering beside the cooker, centimetres from a red-hot ring. A pan lay on its side by her feet and a mess of splattered boiled potatoes and steaming water spread out from it. Her father, his right hand raised and clasped into a fist, towered over her.

Eli jumped between Emma and her dad, pushing her away, as the tight fist landed. I heard the thwack as Eli's head jerked to the side, blood spattering from his burst lip.

"No!" I lurched towards Eli but the look in his eyes reminded me of his instructions so, instead of helping him, I rushed forwards, my feet sliding on the wet floor, and grabbed Emma's arm.

Feeling like I was tearing my heart from my body, I yelled, "Come on!" and dragged Emma towards the door.

"What ...?" she cried but was too surprised to resist and allowed me to pull her from the kitchen and down the hall.

As we raced out to the street, questions bombarded my mind; what would happen to Eli? Would he be killed? The image of the fist smashing into his gorgeous face and the blood spurting seared my mind. My stomach felt like a gymnast was doing cartwheels inside it and I clamped my lips tight to keep from being sick. Pushing the image from my mind, I ran down the street, dragging Emma with me, until my arm jerked back and I was brought to a sudden stop. I spun round expecting to see Emma's father towering above me but he wasn't there, instead Emma stared at me as though I was an alien.

"Where did you come from?"

I bit my lip. What was I supposed to say? We've come from the past because someone in the future wants to save you? Yeah, sure.

"How did you know where I live?"

"I, er ... thought you might be in trouble," I said. "I followed you earlier. I was worried about you."

Emma assessed me for a minute then nodded. She glanced nervously back towards the house.

"Who's that boy?"

"He's my boyfriend." *Why did I say that? Why was that the first thing that came into my mind?*

"He's still there." She chewed her thumb again as she gazed back up the road.

"He'll be okay," I said, hoping it was true.

"But Dad's ... dangerous."

I swallowed.

"He'll be all right," I said again, wishing I believed it. Realistically, I had no idea what Eli could handle but I remembered his nervous look before we went into the house and the gymnast in my stomach did several back-flips.

"We should go back," Emma said, her face pale.

"Do you really want to?"

She stared at the pavement and scuffed her soft, blue pumps. "It's not Dad's fault for being angry. I dropped the potatoes; he's been at work all day and needs his dinner."

"Everyone makes mistakes, Emma."

"But I'm always making them."

"Probably because your dad makes you nervous."

Emma was silent for so long I didn't know whether to speak or let her think. My mind slipped back to the house and Eli, hoping he was okay.

"Dad'll be so mad with you two charging in," she said, eventually. "He's gonna go ballistic." She raised her head, her hand covering her mouth and tears running freely down her cheeks. "I'm scared, Jess."

"Do you want to call for help?" I asked, quietly.

Emma paused, but only for a second, before nodding.

"I was going to go out after tea and call them but now he's too mad, I'll be grounded."

Her bottom lip trembled and more tears streamed down her already-wet face. Her nose ran too and I fished a tissue from my pocket.

"I don't know what he'll do if I go back." She wiped her eyes then blew her nose.

"Do you want me to dial the number for you?"

She nodded again. I pulled my mobile out of my backpack and dialled 0800 1111 then handed the phone to Emma.

After a slight pause she said, "Hello," in a soft, almost inaudible voice.

I couldn't hear the other side of the conversation but from Emma's answers I could guess the questions they were asking.

"I don't want to go home."

"Because my dad gets angry."

"Yes. Some friends came and got me out."

"One's with me here, the other's still with my dad."

"I think so, he's real mad."

As the conversation continued Emma gradually opened up; she seemed glad to finally tell someone official.

After giving our current location Emma finally said, "Thank you," and handed the mobile back to me.

"They were real nice," she said, "They didn't push me to say more than I wanted. Do you think I've done the right thing?"

"Definitely."

"A social worker's coming to get me."

"Is that okay with you?" I asked.

Emma nodded. "I don't want to be scared anymore. I told them I want to live with my mum if they can find her. They said I'll go into foster care, for now, until they can look into it."

"What if they can't find her?" I asked, wanting to prepare her, just in case.

"Then I still won't go back to Dad, at least, I don't think so, I don't know. They said I had a right to feel safe. Do you believe that?"

I nodded.

"But I still love my dad."

I didn't really understand how she could love somebody who violently beat her but I could see the conflict in her eyes. I guess, no matter what he'd done, he was still her dad and she loved him but feared him at the same time.

"I told them about your friend. They asked if I thought Dad would hurt him and I said 'yes' so they're sending the police. I shouldn't have said that, now I've got dad in trouble."

I'd been trying to focus on helping Emma but her words brought my fear for Eli to the front of my mind again. What had happened to him? Shouldn't he be out of the house by now, if he was safe? At least the police would help him when they arrived but would they get there soon enough and what would he tell them? He couldn't exactly say he went into the house because of loud music and he definitely couldn't say he knew what was happening because he works for a futuristic agency ... that's if he could talk at all ...

"Emma, you did the right thing. You told the truth. Look, are you okay waiting here for the social worker while I go back and check on Eli?"

Emma's eyes widened.

"But what will I say to them? And what if Dad comes?"

"He won't, we'll make sure of that." I tried to sound confident but for all I knew Eli could be unconscious, or worse, and her dad could already be on his way. Instinctively, I glanced up the road, half expecting to see her dad charging towards us. Thankfully, the road was empty but was that a good thing? Where was Eli?

My feet shuffled, wanting to go but feeling tied to Emma; I didn't want her to change her mind.

"You'll be fine," I said, half to re-assure myself. "The social worker will be lovely but I really have to go help Eli now."

"Okay," she said, her voice quivering, "Go help your boyfriend. Don't let my dad hurt him."

I touched her arm, gave a quick nod, then set off running down the road. About half way there I paused and glanced back to make sure Emma wasn't following but she hadn't moved. She stood, motionless, watching me go.

I raised my arm, hoping I was doing the right thing. If Emma changed her mind because I'd left her I could be putting her life back in danger but I couldn't abandon Eli. He could be the one receiving the fatal beating.

***

CHAPTER SEVEN - POLICE

The sound of distant sirens pushed me back into action. Eli could not be in the house when the police arrived.

Crashing through Emma's gate, I raced up the drive but as I reached the door it burst open and Eli ploughed into me. All the air exploded from my lungs as I fell back and Eli landed on top of me.

Eli recovered first. He pushed himself up then grabbed my arm and pulled me up too.

"Come on, he could be right behind me and I can hear sirens, we've got to get out of here!"

Yeah, like I hadn't noticed!

The sirens were coming from our left so he turned right out of the gate and ran towards Emma. His long legs easily out-strode mine, even though his steps were uneven.

Ahead, a small silver car stood next to the pavement with the front passenger door open. A tall woman in faded jeans and leather jacket stood talking to Emma.

"I can't go yet; I've got to know if they're …" Emma peered around the woman at the sound of our hurried footsteps and her worried frown morphed into a smile. "You're okay!"

"Yeah, we're fine," I said, grinning up at Eli. But I was surprised to see him frowning.

"Are you Emma's friends?"

"Yes," I answered.

"Hello, I'm Marion Weatherall, I'm a social worker. Thank you for helping Emma."

"That's okay," I said, wondering why Eli stood stiff beside me. "You got here quickly."

"I was on stand-by and fortunately, I live fairly close by. Look, you seem to be in a hurry but you really need to speak to the police and tell them what's happened. They'll need your names and addresses, as well." She looked at Eli's split bottom lip, "And it looks like you will need to be checked out, young man."

The siren, which had been growing louder, suddenly stopped. I looked over my shoulder and watched as a police car pulled up outside Emma's house and two officers spilled out.

"Do you want me to come with you?" Marion offered but glanced at Emma, as though trying to decide her priority.

"No, that's okay," Eli said. "I think Emma would prefer you stay with her. We'll go back now." He gave her one of his winning smiles and she visibly relaxed.

"Are you ready then Emma?"

Emma looked up the road, her forehead creased and her bottom lip trembling.

"They won't hurt my dad, will they?" she asked, her voice so vulnerable she sounded like a five-year-old.

"No, they won't hurt him," Marion said, "But they will have to question him."

"It'll be fine," I said, hoping I was right.
Emma nodded.

"Will I see you again?" she asked.

"I don't know but, don't worry, everything will work out okay."

We hugged then Emma climbed in the passenger seat.

"Come on then," Eli said, turning back towards the house. He walked slowly as the social worker went around the bonnet of her car and climbed into the driver's seat. I heard the door slam and the engine start.

"We're not really going back, are we?" I asked.

"No, but we've got to make the social worker think we are," Eli hissed.

"We're half way there," I said, as the car still idled behind us.

Another police car drove up and stopped behind the first one. Eli slowed his pace further, any slower and we'd be going backwards.

"You're limping," I said, noticing it even more now.

"I'll be fine. Right now, I'm just bothered about avoiding the police."

"What if they do see us, can't we just say we stopped to help?" I asked.

"They'll want our details and they'll speak to our parents. It'll be a big surprise to your mum to find out you were here and probably at home at the same time."

I frowned.

"I'd be at school."

"Time travel?"

"Oh, yeah."

We'd gone forward in time to next Thursday evening when I'd normally be in my bedroom doing my homework.

"I guess it'd be a problem with your parents, as well."

"There's only my mum and she'd freak out, especially if the police mention my age."

"Oh yeah. How old are you and how old should you be on this date?"

"Nice try."

"Aw, come on, you said you'd tell me later. This is later."

"Not later enough."

"Come on, you can tell me."

"You know I can't."

I frowned up at him and knew there was no point pushing; I'd get more out of a mime artist.

Ahead of us the two new officers stepped out of their car. We were only a few metres away and our pace had slowed almost to a stop.

Finally, the social worker's car revved and pulled out into traffic. We waved to Emma, her face a mixture of hope and worry, as they passed. The brake lights came on at the end of the road then turned right. Emma had gone.

"Run!" Eli hissed, grabbing my arm and spinning me around. My legs platted and I stumbled. Waving my free arm, I managed to steady myself and follow him, as the two new officers glanced in our direction then walked towards the house.

We pounded down the street and didn't stop until we'd turned a couple more corners and knew we weren't being followed.

"Okay, we can walk now," Eli panted. "Try to look casual."

Oh yeah, like I could look casual while panting like a thirsty dog. I was sure my face must have been bright red from running away like two escaped criminals and Eli's limp was much worse.

I was desperate to ask what had happened in the house and how soon we'd know Emma's future but I was too busy gasping for breath. Right then, I decided I needed to take up sport, jogging probably, if I was gonna carry on working with it Eli.

***

"So, tell me." I'd been sitting on the bus long enough to get my breath back and was ready for some answers. "What happened in the house and what happened to your leg? I've seen the limp."

"Not here."

I was about to argue but noticed a young kid, about five-years-old, kneeling beside his mum and starring at us over the back of his seat. Had he seen us when we sat up after our time slip and realised we'd just appeared?

"Okay, so tell me why we ran away. We'd have looked less suspicious if we'd walked," I whispered.

"The first officers had been in the house a while, long enough to secure Emma's dad; I'm sure Emma will have said I was there with her dad ..."

"Yeah, she did."

"So, when they didn't find me, one of them could have come out looking for me, at any minute; they could even have radioed the second pair to be on the look out for me. It was best to put as much distance as possible between them and us, before that happened, so there'd be no awkward questions."

"Oh."

It was hard to wait until the journey was over to ask more but as soon as we stepped off the bus, I was ready.

"Okay, tell me now."

Before Eli could answer, my ears tweaked at the distant sound of the school bell.

"Looks like the Watchers got us back on time, after all," Eli said.

"So long as it's not the bell for break," I muttered. "But you've still got to tell me what happened. I can't wait until after school."

"Sorry, Jess, I've my own bus to catch."

"Where to?"

He smiled.

Well, it was worth a try.

"What about your cheek?" I asked, staring at the bruise spreading across the left side of his face.

"I've explained away worse injuries. I'll meet you after school and bring you up to speed. I should have an update on Emma then as well."

"Can't you come at lunch?"

"I'll ask."

School seemed so unimportant, compared to finding out about Emma, but I had no choice. I crossed the road then glanced back but Eli had already gone.

"Where'd you go so quickly?" I muttered.

Then I spotted him, settling into a seat on a single decker bus, heading towards town. I ran back to see the destination on the front.

"Rotherham," I read aloud but it didn't tell me much. At Rotherham bus station, he could catch another to Sheffield or anywhere. As the bus pulled out, I saw Eli smiling at me and shaking his head. I stuck out my tongue, only to see his grin widen. So, he'd caught me snooping; he should just tell me about himself then I wouldn't have to snoop.

I jogged into school, trying to work out excuses for being late and hoping it really wasn't the bell for break. I made a mental note to find out the correct time and alter my watch which, because of my trip, read 11 am. I just hoped the day would be straight-forward and easy.

How is it that you never seem to get what you want?

***

Thankfully, it wasn't break but I was late for registration and Mrs Smith didn't buy my excuse of mum overlaying.

"You are nearly fifteen-years-old and shouldn't have to rely on your mother to get you up in a morning," she said, while scraping her long black hair behind her ear. "There's been a wonderful invention, in fact, it's been around a while, called an alarm clock. Learn to use one." She sighed. "As it's the first time you've been late, I will let you off with a warning, this time. However, if it happens again I will be giving you detention and that will mean ringing your mother. Do you think she'll agree that it's her fault you're late?"

"No, Miss."

"Very well, take your seat and don't let it happen again."

Queenie looked at me, her eyebrows raised, as I took my seat beside her.

"It must be getting serious with Eli if you risk a detention for ten minutes with him," she whispered.

I just shrugged, if she only knew what I'd just been doing and that I'd actually been gone for over two hours.

My next problem came in history.

"Jess Hardwick, I asked you a question!"

Wrenched from my thoughts about Emma, my head jerked up at the sound of my name. Everyone turned towards me, making my cheeks burn. I gazed at Mrs Hatherley and the board behind her for a clue.

'Augustus' was written at the top then 'Julius'. Did she want to know who came next or what they had in common?

Hoping for the best, I said, "Caesar, Miss?"

Laughter fluttered around the room like hundreds of butterflies and Mrs Hatherley's shoulders stiffened. Mine sagged.

"Jessica, that was our topic ten minutes ago. Have you any idea what we are actually talking about now?"

Not the foggiest, but I didn't say that, I just tried to look as intelligent as my silence would let me.

"You don't, do you? Where are you today?"

Okay, so that's one of those stupid questions, teachers ask, that have no right answer and Mrs Hatherley was actually waiting for one! I paused for as long as my nerves would allow and when she still stared at me, I said.

"Here, Miss?"

"Don't try to be clever, Jessica Hardwick, it doesn't suit you."

Told you, no right answer, but isn't being clever what we're actually here for?

"You had better start paying attention," she continued, "Or you'll find yourself in detention."

That woke me up; that was the second warning of detention in one day! I've never been threatened with one before, not ever. They couldn't keep me for more than ten minutes without giving mum advanced notice but they'd still ring her and, knowing mum, she'd tell them that, if I deserved it, they should keep me for the maximum time allowed today and not put it off until tomorrow. She'd then demand a full explanation when I got home and I didn't have one, not one she'd believe anyway. Not only that, being kept after school meant I'd miss Eli and I wouldn't find out about Emma or what happened between Eli and Emma's dad.

I sat up quickly and focussed on history. Whenever a picture of Eli or Emma crept into my mind, I pushed it away.

When lunchtime came, I didn't look for any of my friends; I just walked through the car park and out the gates, hoping Eli would be there early. Maybe he'd already found out about Emma and had come to tell me straight away to stop me worrying.

I looked towards his normal position but my hope sagged like a flat tyre; he wasn't there. With only a tiny slice of hope left, I scanned further up the road.

'Yes!' Joy jumped into my throat so fast I nearly choked. He was there, about twenty metres away, talking to a girl wearing our uniform.

My smile changed to a frown. Who was he talking to? I thought I was the only one he worked with here. And why would he meet her first when he knew how desperately I needed to know about Emma?

The girl stood with her back to me, chatting animatedly, her arms making graceful gestures. It didn't take much knowledge of body language to pick up that she fancied him. Her slim hips tipped from side to side and her long, blonde hair frequently flicked over her shoulders. I bet she was even fluttering her eyelashes, the flirt!

What if she's his girlfriend? She looks about his age and they're standing pretty close.

My chest contracted, but why? What did I care? He could go out with whoever he wanted. We worked together, that's all; but it didn't stop me glaring at the girl's back.

What's wrong with me?

As I watched, his face lit up and he nodded, smiling. He touched the girl's arm and she melted. She dipped towards him then placed her hand on his, lingering. He took his hand away as she turned towards me.

Time froze and my heart actually stopped beating.

The girl's beautiful face shone. A self-satisfied smile, perfectly shaped, played on her lips and her blue eyes sparkled.

It was Lisa.

***

CHAPTER EIGHT - LISA

Why are you talking to her? Do you fancy her? She's vicious and mean but, well, gorgeous, I guess. But I thought you'd want more than just looks. I thought you were better than that.

Bitter thoughts engulfed me but I didn't have time to wallow in them; springing back to life, I dodged back through the school gates before Lisa saw me.

I could actually taste bile in my throat and was glad I hadn't eaten lunch yet. The CLC (City Learning Centre) block stood beside the gates and I hid behind it, waiting until Lisa passed.

She strolled by, her head high, looking confident and assured like she owned the whole world. Well, it definitely looked like she owned Eli.

I stepped from behind the building and through the gates, as soon as Lisa was out of sight, but Eli had gone.

Pain spread through my chest. He'd come to see Lisa, not me. He must have known her all along. I bet they enjoyed planning my beating. It was probably Lisa's idea or maybe it was Eli's. My enthusiasm for him, the Time Agency and the mission snuffed out like a campfire in the rain.

I'll find out about Emma's new future then tell Eli where to stick his job.

Dragging myself back into school, I headed for the café. I didn't really feel like eating but some fuel was needed to keep my brain working for the rest of the day.

"Hey," Queenie said as I joined them, at the edge of the café, with my under-laden tray, "Not seen you in here lately."

"You wouldn't have today either," I said, "Except my mind was on meltdown this morning and I forgot to make sandwiches."

"It was on meltdown in history, as well," Queenie said. "I mean, Mrs Hatherley had only been going on about Nero and the Christians for, like, ten minutes before asking for your opinion on why he blamed them for the fire."

I shrugged.

"Well, you'd better get your head straight," Tammy announced. "Cos you've got French this afternoon and if Mr Frederique catches you day dreaming you'll get twice the homework and a week's detention."

"Mr Frederique gives detentions out like sweets," Leah added.

I sighed. At that minute, I couldn't care a toss about Mr Frederique or homework or detention. What did any of it matter, anyway?

"Move! Now!"

The icy voice meant to freeze any resistance had the opposite effect.

Heat flushed through my body so fast my eyes probably flashed red. Spinning around, I looked up into Lisa's supercilious face.

"Don't you ever get fed up?" I snapped. "Every dinnertime you cruise the dining room, swinging your hips, looking for somebody to pick on just to prove you're 'it'. Well, you're not, okay?" A gasp spread around the nearest tables. "Anyone who has to prove their 'power' everyday is obviously an insecure, power crazy, tyrant who probably got beaten up once too often in primary school. Well, get over it! You're nearly grown up now and it's time to start acting like a human being!"

Lisa didn't need to say anything.

It was Deja Vue as lanky Melissa and 'BJ' Becky grabbed my arms and yanked me out of my chair so fast the backs of my legs burned.

The earlier heat left me, as quickly as it came, and now I wished I'd kept my big mouth shut.

"March!" Lisa hissed in my ear.

I could have said 'No', and shouted for help, but I didn't want double payback later. It was easier to take a painless dunking now than another beating after school.

"Oh, dear," Lisa said, loudly enough for any staff to hear, "Jess looks a bit sick; we'd better help her to the toilets."

Her third friend, Alana, grinned as they led me from the room.

"Look, she's scared," lanky Melissa crowed as we entered the corridor and the café doors swung shut behind us.

"In your dreams," I said, while looking up the stairs and hoping Mrs Quinn would save me again but, no such luck this time, there was no sign of any teachers.

I know a dunking doesn't actually hurt but it is embarrassing. I could hardly be 'tough me' with my hair dripping toilet water down my neck. It gives a whole new meaning to 'eau de toilet'.

The ladies' door crashed against the wall with the enthusiastic push of 'BJ' Becky.

My brain scrambled for a solution as the toilets loomed and, panicking, I said the first thing that popped into my head.

"So, how do you know Eli?"

"What?" Lisa said as Becky and Melissa pushed me into the nearest cubicle and squeezed in behind me.

"You heard," I said, as confidently as I could with a stained white bowl yawning before me.

"What do you know about Eli?" Lisa asked, from outside the cubicle, while hands gripped the back of my neck. I couldn't even fight back; each girl had one of my arms pinned behind my back while they used their other to force my head further down.

"Let me up and I'll tell you," I said then clamped my lips together as my head descended into the reeking hole.

"No way," said Melissa, leaning against me as she reached forward to flush.

"What do you know about Eli?" Lisa demanded.

"Mn hmn." I shook my head; there was no way I'd open my mouth with Melissa about to give me a shower. I heard the metal rattle and closed my eyes, taking a deep breath.

"Let her up!"

"What?" Becky exclaimed.

"I said, let her up."

Becky tutted and Melissa groaned as they pulled my head out of the toilet bowl and I finally dared to breathe.

"Let her go," Lisa ordered.

I was still bent double, facing the toilet, so couldn't see their faces but I could imagine their expressions.

"I said, let her go!"

Their grip relaxed then released me. I straightened up and brought my arms back to their normal position, rubbing my aching muscles.

"Now, get outside!"

No one moved. I dared a look over my shoulder.

Lisa stood, hands on narrow hips, frowning in my direction. Melissa and Becky both stood like mindless drones, staring at their leader in confusion.

"I said, 'outside'. Now!"

Finally, my two jailers shuffled out of the cubicle, giving Lisa a quizzical look, and I finally had enough room to turn around. I watched them leave, followed by Alana, and the outer toilet door swung shut behind them.

Before I had chance to do or say anything, Lisa pounced. She sprang forwards, like a panther, grabbed the collar of my school shirt and slammed me back against the toilet tank.

Pain shot through my upper back and my legs buckled. I was almost sitting on the toilet, only her iron grip kept me from sinking down onto it.

"Now, tell me. What do you know about Eli?"

***

CHAPTER NINE – SUSPICIONS

"Not much," I choked out, which was true, "I've talked to him a bit and I saw you talking to him today."

"Did you hear what we said?"

"No."

Lisa's grip eased a bit but not much.

"So, what have you talked to him about?"

"A girl he knows who needs help; he's worried about her, is all." I figured a bit of truth would keep me on track and hopefully satisfy her.

"A girl who needs help? What's her name?"

"Emma."

Lisa's hands dropped but she continued to lean over me, examining me, like a squashed bug on a windscreen. I was still plastered against the toilet and wishing she'd let me move.

"You?" Her lip curled as she spoke. "It can't be."

"It can't be me, what?"

"They wouldn't choose a nobody like you," Lisa muttered, backing out of the cubicle and looking at me like she'd just found a maggot in her sandwich. "You're just a meddler who thinks you're some kind of agony aunt to your 'so-called' friends." She laughed, a wicked, fit-for-an-evil-queen laugh. "They're such good friends they stand by and let you get dunked."

Okay, that hurt; the truth does. I always try to be there for my friends but when it comes to tackling

Lisa they're never there for me. Although, to be fair, they do constantly warn me not to wind her up.

"Is it you?"

"I am me, yes." *Ok, she's officially losing it.*

"No, you know what I mean."

"Actually, no, I don't."

I jumped as Lisa's fist slammed against the cubicle wall.

"I'm going to find out if it's you, and if it is, then I'm going to sort it." She spun around and marched out of the toilets.

I stood there as the door swung shut.

What was that? What was she going on about? Is she coming back?

I peeked out of the cubicle. The toilets were empty.

Has she really gone or is she waiting outside? Buy why? What did she mean 'she's going to find out if it's me'? She knows it's me; I was standing right in front of her. Who else would she bring to the toilets for a shower date? Or maybe, there's so many of us, she's losing track? But, why didn't she know who I am? She's the one who brought me in here. And what's she going to sort?

I tiptoed to the door and slowly eased it open, just enough to let one eye peer through the gap. Nothing. I opened it a bit further and stuck my head out. There were a few people in the corridor but no sign of Lisa or her cronies.

I let out the breath I'd been holding and stepped into the corridor.

"Jess!" I spun around expecting to be slammed back into the ladies for my early shower but instead my timorous friends came hurtling towards me.

"You haven't been dunked. Again," said Tammy, examining my head as though checking for head lice.

"There's no need to sound so disappointed."

"What happened?" asked Leah.

"I honestly have no idea."

My friends gave me a disbelieving look and insisted on the details. I told them everything except the part about Emma. They looked at me as though I'd grown two heads.

"Don't look at me like that. I told you, I've no idea what happened."

"Whatever, but I reckon you'd better watch your back and keep out of her way," Queenie instructed.

"I intend to."

I spent the rest of the day on high 'Lisa alert' in case she came to her senses and decided to pick up where she'd left off. But, after ducking around a couple of corners at speeds a jaguar would envy, I actually managed to keep out of her way.

By the time the final bell rang I was exhausted but I still dodged out before my friends. I even mumbled something about being in a hurry and left Leah packing up her French exercise books alone. I needed to see Eli and find out about Emma before Lisa had chance to grab him again.

Wishing I had spidey senses, I crossed the car park and peered out through the gates. Eli stood alone but on my right this time, as casual as ever, leaning against the railings, one leg crossed over the other. Dressed in ripped jeans and black hoody, he lazily watched a dozen lads, with their school jumpers tied around their waists, playing football on the field opposite. Goodness knows how they'd got out there so quickly.

Marching up to him, I ducked forward to peek beneath his hoody. His left cheek had already bruised black and his top lip on that side was twice its normal size. If it wasn't for seeing him with Lisa earlier, and knowing he'd been lying to me, I would have felt sorry for him but, at the moment, any sympathy was squashed beneath the anger I was trying to keep hidden.

I'd decided to keep my knowledge to myself until he'd told me about Emma then I'd challenge him about his lies.

"Hi."

"Hi," he said and leaned to his right so that he could still see the game.

"That looks painful."

"Hmn?" He pulled his eyes towards me so slowly it was like they were battling a force field.

"I said, 'that looks painful'."

"Oh, it's okay, hurts a bit but not bad."

His eyes drifted back to the game.

I couldn't believe this; he was supposed to be delivering really important news and he was too busy watching some lads kick a football about. Boys!

"That ginger kid is a fantastic player," he said, "He just dribbled right past that huge skinhead."

"Yeah, right, that's just what I need to know. Eli! What happened to Emma?"

Slowly he dragged his eyes back to mine.

"Oh, Emma's fine."

Air rushed out of me like a released balloon. I hadn't realised how much I'd been holding my breath.

"So, what happened?"

"Well, technically, it's 'what happens?' Right now, she's still with her dad."

I frowned trying to get my exhausted brain cells around the time changes but quickly gave up. I'll never figure out this time travel business.

"Anyway," Eli continued, "Emma stays in care for twelve months but they finally track down her mother in Cornwall. She's remarried with a baby daughter. She's a bit reluctant to take on Emma, at first, thinking her new husband might not like it. But, in the end, it's her second husband who persuades her to let Emma come."

"Does that work out okay?"

"Yeah, I guess it must have been awkward at first but records show Emma's okay. She gets all A*s, goes to university and studies medicine. She becomes a doctor, specialising in paediatrics. Over the years, she spots the signs and helps three other kids escape abusive parents."

"Wow, so we've really helped four people?" A wonderful, warm glow spread from my heart and around my whole body.

"And more, probably. Who knows how many those other three will go on to help?"

"But I thought the Time Watchers make sure that our actions don't alter their time too much?"

"Any changes we make now are bound to alter the future. They just try to choose people where the changes will be good, and not too massive, but there are no guarantees."

"Has it ever gone wrong?"

Eli watched the football as he spoke. "Once or twice I think but, like I said before, they're not so far in the future so any changes aren't catastrophic."

"How far are they?"

"I don't know, and before you say anything, I have asked. Zac's so … futuristic. I figured he was from centuries ahead so the changes we made would be huge. Anyway, when I asked him, he just grinned and said, 'technology advances quickly, so does fashion. What you think will take centuries may only take a few generations,' or something like that."

"So, it could be, like, our grandchildren who are the Watchers?"

Eli shrugged. "Or thereabouts. I pushed but he wouldn't tell me any more. They don't like us knowing too much about the future."

I let that sink in before asking my next question.

"So, what happens to Emma's birth dad?"

"He doesn't serve any time thanks to us intervening."

"But he was going to hit her and he did hit you!" I couldn't believe he got off.

"But I can't press charges, can I?" He shrugged. "That's how it goes. Anyway, he never marries again. He lives with a woman for a couple of years but she leaves him saying his temper is out of control. He lives alone after that. It doesn't matter, we did good, we saved Emma and now we have another assignment."

"Another one? Already? I thought you said they take it easy and check everything out first?"

So much for sorting Leah out once my head was free of Emma.

"They do, but it could have been weeks, months or even years for them."

I let my fried brain slowly soak that up.

"Wait a minute, you haven't told me what happened between you and Emma's dad yet."

Eli shrugged. "Nothing."

"Eli!" He was the most infuriating boy I'd ever met. "Tell me!"

"Ah, so this is why you rushed off and left me in French." Leah's voice broke through my focus on Eli. I turned and saw her approaching with Jake glued to her hip. Queenie and Tammy followed, also glued to their boyfriends.

"Oh look, it's the Chav," Jake sneered.

"Hi Leah," I said, ignoring Jake. "Yeah, sorry about that."

"Well," said Tammy, her eyebrows raised. "Aren't you going to introduce us?"

"Eli, this is Queenie, Tammy, Leah, Dwaine, Chad and Jake. Everyone, this is Eli."

"Hi," everyone but Jake echoed.

"Hi," Eli replied.

"So, you're the new boyfriend," Queenie said.

"He's not my boyfriend!" I protested while Eli looked at me, his eyebrows raised. He didn't seem too upset though, in fact, there was a slight smile trying to escape his lips.

The girls looked at each other, grinning.

This is so awkward, hurry up and go home!

Tammy picked up on my silent vibes. "Well, I guess we'd better leave you two love-birds…" I scowled at her. "Sorry, non-love-birds to do whatever you're gonna do or not do." Tammy winked, "See you tomorrow, Jess."

"Yeah, see you," I groaned, knowing they would wind me up.

She set off with Dwaine, Queenie and Chad followed, Leah and Jake were last.

"Tell me all about it tomorrow," Leah whispered as she passed.

I closed my eyes. Could this day get any more embarrassing?

"Sorry about that," I said, turning back to Eli, "They like to wind me up, they didn't mean anything."

Eli just grinned and shrugged.

"So, you were about to tell me about this morning, what happened with Emma's dad. Tell me everything; don't leave anything out."

"It was nothing."

"That's not nothing," I said, pointing to his cheek.

Eli's mood changed; his smile slid away, he sighed and shoved his hands into his pockets.

"Alright, if you really want to know…"

"Yes, I really want to."

His eyes focussed somewhere over my shoulder but not at the game.

"Okay, so you saw me … get hit. Yeah?"

I nodded.

"Well, it felt like my face exploded and I fell. Hot water soaked into my trousers but at least it wasn't scolding. Her dad shouted at me, demanding to know who I was and kicking me with every other word. I couldn't defend myself on the floor so I got up, as soon as I could, and tried to tell him I was Emma's friend, and didn't want any trouble, but he just kept yelling that he didn't believe me." Eli looked down at the ground and carried on, his voice softer. "His face was red and his eyes bulged like a madman. I pushed him away and tried to get past him but he grabbed my arm and slammed me against the kitchen units. He was still yelling, demanding to know about me and Emma. He thought we were an item and said some really vile stuff. I tried to pull his hands off me but that only made it worse. He got hold of the neck on my hoody and pulled it tight."

I stood there, amazed. Eli had gone through all this and afterwards acted like everything was okay.

"He was completely off his head. He kept screaming about Emma being a slut, like her mother, and demanded to know about me and her. I told him there was nothing between us but he was having none of it. In the end his grip was so tight I couldn't speak." Eli fell silent, his jaw working. When he started talking again, his voice was so quiet, I had to lean in to hear him.

"I was starting to feel light-headed; my chest hurt from lack of air." He paused. "I thought I was gonna die." He stopped speaking for so long I couldn't stand it.

"And?" I urged. "What did you do?"

"I was close to passing out and knew, if that happened, I probably wouldn't get out of there so I kneed him in the b ... well, you know. He yelled and let go of me. I took my chance, shoved him away and legged it. That's when I ran into you."

"Literally."

"Ugh?"

"Never mind."

Eli's jaw worked a bit more then his gaze drifted back to the game behind me.

I let him watch them for a minute while I watched him. He'd risked his life for Emma and only just made it out. He was amazing, a real hero; compared to him, I'd done nothing. With all those kicks, it was no wonder he had a limp when he came out. His legs were probably covered in bruises.

I knew I still needed to tackle him about Lisa but his story had soaked up most of my anger. How could I have a go at someone so selfless? Instead, I tried a safer subject and stepped into his line of sight again.

"Eli, please stop watching the game and tell me what our next mission is."

"Oh, yeah, right." He refocused.

"Well, there's this kid, Liam, he's the oldest of three brothers. He's fourteen, Ashley's twelve and Kian's four. Because Liam's the eldest he always gets stuck looking after Kian."

"What about their parents?"

"Their dad's a truck driver and away a lot. Their mother works until late, most days. That's why Liam gets to be babysitter."

"I bet he hates that."

The thought of having my kid sister hanging around, wherever I went, made me shudder. She could be a real pain-in-the-neck, when she wanted to be, and I could imagine what my friends would say. They'd probably ditch me as well as my sister. There were conversations us girls shared that no ten-year-old should hear.

"Yeah, and that's the problem. In three months, Kian throws a tantrum in front of Liam's friends. Liam tells the kid to get lost. He walks away with his friends expecting Kian to follow."

"But he doesn't." A sickly feeling stirred in my stomach.

"No, he doesn't. Liam only leaves him about five minutes but when he goes back Kian is gone. He's never seen again."

"Never?"

Eli shook his head. "No one knows what happened to him. He's not picked up on any CCTV footage, or anything. Liam's mother blames him; she never forgives him and he never forgives himself. He ends up in all sorts of bother, gets into drugs and dies in his late twenties. Their father blames their mother, saying she shouldn't have done so much overtime, and they get divorced. Ashley just slips by everyone's attention; he gets into trouble and spends his life in and out of prison."

"Wow." What else could I say? I mean, one tiny bit of human weakness, not being able to cope and acting like, well, a fourteen-year-old, wrecks five people's lives. No wonder Liam burns out.

"What can we do? Do we go to the time Kian disappears and make sure nobody takes off with him? Or do we rescue him from whoever snatches him?"

"No one knows who snatches him."

"The Watchers must know."

"No, they don't, like I said, there's no CCTV footage found and no witnesses. The Watchers say, his body was never found, so there's no evidence. They don't know whether someone changed his appearance and brought him up as their own; I guess, if that happened, he must forget his childhood or they keep him prisoner or tell him his parents died ... who knows? Or he was killed and buried somewhere but no one finds the remains."

I swallowed. "Who could hurt a little four-year-old kid?"

Eli just looked at me. "Seriously? We live in a warped world, Jess."

"Too warped. So, what can we do?"

"We have to get Liam to want Kian around."

"No way! How can we manage that one? We just need to follow whoever it is or stop Kian running away."

"We're not allowed to interfere like that, remember? People have to make their own choices."

"But he's only four!"

"I know, but if we keep him safe this time, what's to stop it happening again? We can't keep turning up."

"Why not?"

Eli sighed. "Because there are others to save, not just Kian. Plus, one of those times we might be too late or have to answer awkward questions from Liam or the police; like how we turn up just when he's running away or someone's in the middle of snatching him. The police might think we have something to do with it. Not to mention the fact that every time we directly intervene, it changes the future. The ripples in time could turn into tidal waves with all the possible outcomes. The Watchers won't sanction that amount of disruption. The best thing is to sort out their relationship, so Kian feels wanted and is watched over properly."

"There's hardly gonna be a queue of people waiting to snatch him."

"No, but one person could be watching and waiting for the right opportunity, a person who will come back if we stop them the first time. Plus, we don't know whether Kian is snatched or whether he runs away and someone spots him and picks him up. We can't just treat the symptoms; we have to treat the illness and that's their relationship."

"Wow, profound or what? So how can we persuade Liam to want him around?"

Eli shrugged. "Not a clue."

"What?"

"Hey, I don't know everything."

Could have fooled me.

"What about the Watchers, don't they know?"

Eli shook his head. "It's like it was with Emma, they can give advice but they can't tell us what will work. They only know the result of what we do after we've done it. Their computer predicts possible outcomes but that's all. They sometimes come up with suggestions, like recruiting you and getting you to talk to Emma because they knew you were gonna get beaten up, but mostly it's up to us. We have to wing it unless the 'go-between' has any ideas."

"So, how did they know I'd be beaten up? It wasn't exactly world news. It was Lisa who told you, wasn't it? Or did you plan it together to get me to work with you?"

"Lisa who? What are you going on about? A teacher noticed your injuries and made a note about them, to keep an eye on you, and that's how the Watchers know."

Mrs Quinn's concerned face sprang to mind but I wasn't convinced; I might not have known Eli very long but this was the first time he'd lied to me; at least, as far as I knew.

The sight of his bruises, and his account about what happened between him and Emma's dad, had softened my anger but knowing he was lying to me hurt enough to fuel it again.

"Who's Lisa? Oh, you know, slim, blonde, drooling all over you at lunch time."

Eli's Adam's apple bobbed.

"That Lisa? You saw us?"

"Yeah, I saw you. In fact, I decided I'd find out about Emma and then quit this whole 'Time Agency' thing."

"You can't do that! You're good at it and I ... people need you!"

"Really? Then stop lying and start telling me the truth about you and the evil queen."

"I don't know what you're talking about. Who's the evil queen and why would you have a problem with me talking to Lisa? I didn't even think you'd know her because she's older than you. Why would me talking to her stop you working for the Agency?"

"Well, for one, you met her instead of me, even though you knew how desperate I was to find out about Emma. Two, why would you have anything to do with a reptile like her? And, three, you told me you didn't know her."

"When?"

"When I went into the park to see Emma; you told me you hadn't made her beat me up to make the mission work but you did, didn't you?"

"What?" Eli's eyes bulged. "That was Lisa? I told you the truth, I didn't organise that, the Watchers just knew it was going to happen. They didn't even know who'd done it. I hated seeing you hurt and I promise you, I didn't even know Lisa back then."

"Back then? Eli, it was only a couple of weeks ago."

"But when I met her today, I didn't recognise her, honest! I didn't know she was the same person! The girls had their backs to me when they were hurting you."

He, sort of, sagged and sighed like he knew he was beaten.

"Okay, look, the people I work for use go-betweens, as I've explained before. My contact is usually Zac but a new pair of Time Fixers has just been set up and Zac got assigned to them because he's got loads of experience. I was only switched to Lisa today.

This lunch was the first time I met her. I honestly didn't recognise her."

I stared at him, trying to work out whether he was telling the truth or not.

"It's true," he said, "Honest."

"So, why would the Watchers use Lisa?" I asked. "She's not exactly a 'helping others' kind of person."

Eli shrugged. "No idea. The Watchers pick go-betweens, train them and assign them. They usually have someone from their own time. I don't know why they'd use someone like Lisa. Unless they don't know what she's like."

"How can they not know? They're in the future."

Eli shook his head, "I don't know, it's weird, unless …"

"Unless what?"

"When she beat you up, is that the only time she's ever done anything like that?"

"No, she's always picking on somebody, beating them up, tearing up their homework …"

Eli frowned. "Does she ever bully online, you know, with facebook, twitter, or anything?"

"No, it's always physical." I laughed. "She's a real hands-on person, is Lisa. She's one of a kind."

Eli nodded. "And do teachers ever get involved?"

"No, she's really careful, the teachers all think she's wonderful and no one ever tells on her because she threatens to beat them up twice as badly if they do. She says she'll still get them even if she's expelled. She's very convincing; no one's dared test her word on that one. I think Mrs Quinn suspects something but she's not found out the truth yet."

Eli smiled, knowingly. "She's smart, I'll give her that."

"Ugh?"

"The Watchers only know what's been recorded in history, whether it's on paper or online. If no teacher ever finds out about her, and she never bullies online, they will only see what *is* recorded."

I stared at him. If he was right then Lisa really was a master schemer. The only comments on record were the teachers' reports saying she was a perfect student, always polite, helpful and a good worker. I bet she never said a wrong word online either. No wonder all her bullying was physical. Everything began dropping into place like an expert on Tetris. I shook my head.

"You've got to tell them what she's really like."

"How? Lisa's my contact now. I can't get in direct touch with the Watchers and the only way I'll see Zac is if they replace Lisa and Zac comes back again."

"Oh, come on, there's got to be a way!"

Eli shook his head, "We'll just have to do this mission and hope Zac's back for the next one."

"And if he's not?"

"I don't know; we'll have to think of something."

I sighed. We didn't have much choice. Kian needed us but I wasn't happy about it, not one little bit.

"So did Lisa tell you how to help Kian?"

"Only that we have to persuade Liam to want him around and maybe tell Kian not to talk to strangers. I think this might be her first time as a go-between because she couldn't come up with much to help us. The Watchers must think I have enough experience to come up with something myself. I guess I'm on my own."

"You're not on your own," I said, "You've got me."

A fantastic smile spread over Eli's face. "Yeah, I've got you; now I'm in real trouble."

"Oy!" I said, thumping his arm. His smile just spread further and something inside my stomach melted. I didn't want it to but I couldn't help it, I really fancied him.

"So, I guess you're not quitting then."

"I guess not."

A thought sprang into my mind and my stomach solidified.

"Does Lisa know I work with you?"

Eli shook his head.

"No. Me and the Watchers are her contacts. You and Lisa are mine. The Watchers try to minimise contacts, especially with new fixers and go-betweens."

"Why?"

Eli shrugged. "I guess, if things don't work out with a new worker, or any worker, the less they know, the better."

"But I've already done one mission. How many missions did you do before you met Zac?"

"I met him on my first mission."

"So why am I different?"

Eli stared down at his trainers. "I met him because my mission went badly wrong."

"How?"

"I can't say."

"Not that again."

"Yes, that again. I'm sorry Jess but a day will come when you'll have the answers to all the questions you've been asking me; it just isn't now. Anyway, like I said, I think this is Lisa's first time as a go-between so they'll not want her to meet many others."

"You're only guessing that it's her first mission."

"I don't have all the answers, Jess, I only met her today. Maybe it's because you go to the same school, they might think it's better for you not to know about each other in case of conflicts or talking in school and being overheard. I don't know."

Conflicts between me and Lisa? Erm, too late! Been there, done that, still doing it.

"It's probably better that she doesn't find out about you being part of the agency."

A picture of the ladies flashed through my mind and Lisa's reaction when I asked her about Eli. I think I might have made a big mistake.

***

CHAPTER TEN – BOYFRIEND?

We walked to the end of Knapton Avenue in silence.
"Meet me after school tomorrow. Hopefully, I'll have thought up a plan by then."

"Okay," I agreed and watched Eli walk away.

He didn't sound too convinced; maybe I could come up with something brilliant? Yeah, and all war might end tomorrow. Not likely.

I thought of nothing else all evening but came up with absolute ziltch. No surprise there then. I was so exhausted, after all the lost sleep worrying about Emma, that my mind was mush and I fell asleep within seconds. All night, invisible enemies chased me around Rawmarsh and, no matter what clever tricks my sleepy brain invented, I couldn't escape my pursuers. When Mum called me up, the next morning, I pulled my duvet over my head, wishing I could hibernate for a year.

At breakfast Abby and Jimmy's voices pounded my brain and as I walked to school thoughts still spun around inside my head like wasps hyped up on berry juice. My feet took me all the way there without consulting my brain, at all. In fact, my distracted cells didn't register my surroundings until my path was blocked by a solid object.

Blinking at the near collision, my eyes travelled up and took in expensive black shoes, slim, shapely legs disappearing into a knee-length, black skirt, a skin-tight, white shirt, highlighting more than ample boobs, and pristine, blonde hair resting obediently on narrow shoulders. It was no surprise that the perfect face belonged to none other than Queen Lisa. With narrowed eyes and lips pressed together, it was obvious I was in trouble. Again.

The whole assessment took less than a second and that's all the time she needed to plant one hand on each of my shoulders and push me against a stone wall. Some sort of prickly bush hung over the top, battling with my hair and snagging my clothes.

Satisfied that I was trapped, Lisa spat out. "Tell me how you know Eli."

Still getting over the shock of coming back to reality with a bump, for once, I couldn't think of a thing to say. I mean, ME, presented with the perfect opportunity to smart-mouth Lisa and not a single thought worked its way from my cotton-wool neurons to my unusually inactive tongue.

"Well?" she demanded, giving my shoulders an extra push.

I cringed as the peaks in the stone wall pushed further into my back.

Come on, brain. Think!

At the edge of my vision, I spotted Tammy and Leah near the school gates, huddled together like they were the ones under attack. Both were watching Lisa and me but, of course, neither of them came to help. They might be my friends but they weren't suicidal. Friendship only goes so far, I guess. At that moment, I wished it went a whole lot further.

Lisa towered over me and it wasn't just because of her heels; she could probably join an Amazon tribe and nobody'd realise she didn't belong.

Another shove on my poor battered shoulders pushed my brain into gear.

"What's it to you?" I snapped, with as much confidence as I could fake.

"Never you mind," Lisa snarled. "Just talk or a trip to the toilets will be fun compared with what I'll do to you."

Now, with most people that'd seem like a pretty hollow threat but I knew Lisa. She could be very inventive when it came to thinking up new punishments.

"I just met him after school one day," I blurted, "Like I said before."

"And?"

"And nothing. We just talked for a couple of minutes. He looked worried so I asked him why; that's when he mentioned this Emma person. That's it. He said he was waiting for somebody."

"You're lying. You're working with him, aren't you?"

The blood in my cheeks heated up and started to burn. Did she have a built-in lie-detector or had she checked with the Watchers after the toilet incident? But, if the Watchers had told her everything then she wouldn't need to ask me, would she? I decided to risk it.

"I'm not lying and what're you talking about? I go to school, not work. In case you haven't noticed, I'm too young to have a job."

She pressed harder, her nails digging into my flesh.

"You know what I'm talking about."

"No, I don't, why don't you spell it out?"

The pressure on my shoulders eased momentarily then increased again. She lowered her face until it was about a centimetre from mine. She was so close I could feel her warm breath on my cheeks. Her breath didn't even smell. Evil people are supposed to have bad breath, aren't they? Garlic, rotten meat, fried toad? But no, Miss Perfect had to have perfect smelling breath as well.

"Yesterday was the first time I've met him so, if you're not working with him, why was he here before yesterday?" she hissed.

My mind did a few acrobatics before deciding that a bit of supreme acting was needed to get her away from me.

"How should I know? Look," I spat, sounding impatient, "I don't know what your problem is about this Eli. All I know is that he said he was waiting for somebody to finish football practice, so I guess you should talk to the boys. Now let me GO!"

It took a few seconds for my words to filter through before she gave me a last, hard push.

"You'd better not be lying, Hardwick, because if I find out you are, you're worse than dead."

She squeezed hard, her finger nails digging well in, before letting me go and walking away.

Tammy and Leah waited until she'd gone into school before rushing towards me.

"What was all that about?" Tammy gasped.

"What did you do to get her all riled up like that?" Leah asked, her eyes huge.

"Don't know," I lied. Lying was becoming a habit since meeting Eli and it was *so* not good. Did that mean working for the agency was bad or was it more like being an undercover cop?

Note to self: figure that one out later.

"Well? What did she say?" Tammy demanded, hands on hips.

The truth or not the truth, that is the question. Lies were way too hard to remember so I decided to try the truth, well, half of it anyway.

"She was asking me about Eli. I think she fancies him and wanted to know why he was talking to me."

"And what did you tell her?" Tammy asked. "You didn't say he was your boyfriend, did you?"

"No, of course not. Why would I? I just talk to him sometimes and that's what I told her."

"That's not what it looked like yesterday," Tammy pushed. "The way you look at each other, talking is not the only thing on your minds."

Why would she say that? Just exactly how do we look at each other? I wish I could record our meetings and watch them back so I'd know what she meant.

"And there's no way you'd rush off and leave me in French just to talk to some random boy," Leah added.

"That's exactly what I did."

"Okay, so what was so important for you to say that you had to leave me behind?"

Okay, now I've dropped myself in it.

"We just talk, that's all."

"About what?" Tammy pushed.

"All sorts."

"Like what?"

"Okay, if I say I like him will you just drop it?"

"No, but it's a start," Tammy said, grinning. "So, you do like him and who wouldn't? He's got to be at least an eight."

"He's not an eight, more like a six," I lied.

"No way!" Tammy screeched. "He's an eight and you know it."

"Six."

"Eight."

"You really fancy him, don't you?" Leah said quietly beside me.

"No. He's just okay."

Leah smiled. "Yes, you do, you just don't want to admit it, to us or yourself."

My shoulders sagged, she'd got me and she knew it. I could never fool Leah. She'd just listen to conversations, hardly say a word, but watch everybody and figure out what they were really saying and thinking.

I leaned back against the wall, defeated. "Okay, he's a nine or maybe a ten. No, a nine."

His looks might be a ten but he lost a point because of his weirdness.

Tammy's eyes sparkled. "You've got it bad."

"No, I haven't, and anyway nothing's coming of it. We're just friends."

"Yeah, whatever," Tammy scoffed.

"We are. Okay?" I pushed away from the wall and set off towards the entrance. Tammy and Leah followed.

"How come he's outside our school all the time and not in uniform?" Leah asked.

"I don't know."

I must stop lying, I must stop lying.

"So where does he go?" asked Tammy. "Or has he been expelled?"

I shrugged. "No, he hasn't been expelled but I don't know any more; I haven't exactly got his life story." Now that was true. "So, let's just leave it, okay?"

"Ew, touchy," said Tammy.

I felt, rather than saw, the look Tammy gave Leah and knew neither of them believed me.

At least the questions stopped for the day and Lisa left me alone as well.

***

At the end of school, I walked to the gates with my friends who grinned knowingly when they saw Eli waiting for me. I glanced around but thankfully there was no sign of Lisa. I had to meet Eli and get out of there fast. It was bad enough my friends thinking there was something going on between us but if Lisa saw us together again … my throat dried up at the thought.

"You want to go shopping this weekend?" Tammy asked.

Actually, I did, but I'd no idea when Eli would want to go see Liam so figured I'd better keep the weekend free, just in case.

"I don't think so, but I'll text you if I change my mind."

"Your loss," Tammy said with a shrug.

"I'll go," said Leah.

"Yep, me too. I'll bet Jess is keeping her weekend free for Mr Hotstuff, over there," Queenie said with a wink.

I wrinkled my nose at her but didn't bother denying it.

"See you Monday then!" Tammy said.

"Yeah, see you Monday!" I replied.

A glance around, confirmed there was still no sign of Lisa, and hurried over to Eli.

"Come on, we've got to go!" I said, grabbing his arm.

"What's the hurry?" he asked, resisting my tugging.

"I'll tell you as we go," I said, pulling harder.

Sighing, Eli allowed me to drag him away down the road. I continually glanced over my shoulder and the last time, just before we lost sight of the school, I was sure I spotted blonde hair. I paused, let go of Eli, and cautiously took a step back.

There were only two lads by the gates and neither had blond hair.

"What's wrong?" Eli asked.

"Nothing," I said, setting off again.

I hope.

***

CHAPTER ELEVEN - LIAM

As we sat upstairs, in the front seat, of a double-decker bus, I brought Eli up to date.

"So, it looks like Lisa suspects we're either a couple or working together but the Watchers haven't confirmed it. Maybe she hasn't talked to them yet. I tried to make it sound as though you were meeting one of the boys on the football team but I don't think she bought it. Basically, she's confused and jealous. She's gonna keep on digging to find out why you were at school before she was your contact and why you were talking to me. If she proves either of her suspicions, she's gonna cause trouble."

"She's jealous?" Eli wore a satisfied grin.
Really?

"Try and see the big picture here."

Eli's face straightened.

"So, you think she'll go after you?"

"Yeah, why do you think I dragged you away from school so fast? It's best if she never sees us together."

"But, as soon as she talks to the Watchers she'll know we're working together. Surely, she can't have a problem with that?"

I shrugged. "She hates me. Maybe working together isn't as bad as us being an item but with Lisa, who knows?"

"Why does she hate you?"

"Because I don't jump when she demands it. Everyone else finds it easier to do what she says but I've never been one to take the easy way out. I answer back and she doesn't like it."

"Then let's hope the Watchers don't tell her anything."

"I just wish you could get in touch with Zac."

"There's no way."

I sighed. "Have you come up with anything to help Liam?"

Eli shook his head. "I think we should just try to make friends with him and see how it goes. Maybe you could pretend to be my younger sister?"

I gave him one of my looks. "You've got to be kidding! I'm fourteen. There's no way I'd go trailing after an older brother."

"You could wipe your makeup off and plait your hair," Eli said, lamely. "Then you'd look younger."

"Yeah, about twelve. That's still too old to be hanging around with an older brother. You're what fifteen, sixteen? It'd be better if I pretend to be your girlfriend."

As soon as the words were out of my mouth, I felt my cheeks heat up, even my ears burned. Why did I say that? Eli stared straight ahead out of the window. He couldn't even look at me. I felt like such an idiot.

"Just pretend; you know? It'll be hard but we could, maybe, pull it off. Or not. Never mind, it was a stupid idea."

Shut up, Jess, you're making it worse! I wished I could just jump out the window and off this stupid bus. *Why can't I learn to keep my mouth shut?*

Finally, after a silence that seemed to go on forever, Eli turned and looked at my burning face. I quickly focussed on my knees with my fists clenched in my coat pockets.

"That's a good idea. It might work."

Every part of me exhaled as I looked up at him. "Really?"

"Yeah. Sounds good. Do you think you can pretend to fancy me?"

Can I ever!

"Er, yeah, I think so," I said, lamely, "What about you?"

Eli shrugged. He was good at that. "Yeah, I think I could pull it off." He had this amused smile like he was enjoying his own private joke.

Yeah, real joke having to pretend he likes me. How to make a girl feel good in one easy lesson; I don't think.

"We're here." Eli stood and led the way out of our seat and down the stairs.

A pinging sound rang in my ears as we reached the bottom and the bus pulled in.

"What day are we on?" I whispered, as we stepped onto the curb.

"The same day you were on," he said, "We haven't travelled in time today, just place."

Oh yeah, we never ducked down in our seats.

I looked around.

"This is Mexborough, isn't it?"

"Yeah."

"My aunt used to live here."

"Oh."

Okay, love your enthusiasm about my personal life.

"So, where do we find Liam?"

"Over there." Eli pointed past a large brick building with evenly spaced windows and a high fence.

I followed his gaze to a row of old terraced houses.

"In one of those?"

"No, the park."

Okay, don't see a park.

We walked past the large building, which looked like some sort of residential home, and onto the side road. The row of terraced houses came to an abrupt end and a park spread out beside them. The road curved away from it and new detached and semi-detached houses lined both sides

"Do we always meet people in parks?"

I could imagine the TV advert: 'Troubled? Juggling problems you can't solve? Go to your local park and your help will come.'

"No, we meet them in different places; it's just a co-incidence about the last two."

We crossed over and entered through an opening shaped, and decorated, like a colourful butterfly. Grass spread back and out towards the right in a large rectangle. A small kiddies' area with climbing bars, bouncy toys and swings lay straight ahead but Eli turned right, towards a hard surface with high wire fences.

As we walked, I felt his arm slip around my waist. Warm tingles spread out from it and travelled up and down my spine. It felt good, safe, warm and exciting.

Jess, it's part of the job. It doesn't mean anything!

"That's Liam shooting baskets over there and that's Kian sitting on the floor in the corner."

Forcing myself to focus, I watched dark-haired Liam bounce a ball between his two friends then leap and throw. He grinned as it swished through the net.

Like his friends, his white school shirt had damp patches under the arms and hung loose at the waist. He was slim, good looking and obviously fit.

"How do you know that one's Liam?"

"Lisa showed me photos."

"Where'd she get them from?"

"They were school photos so I guess the Watchers must have got them from archives, or something."

"Oh."

Eli lead me past Liam and over to the other side of the hardcore area. A sea of grass spread out on the other side of the fence with a rocket-shaped climbing frame a short distance away. The ground fell away after that to what looked like a skateboard park but I couldn't really tell as most of was hidden below the slope.

"Not a bad place," I muttered, trying to break some of the tension forming in my stomach. I mean, yeah, it was great having Eli's arm around me but what were we supposed to do next? Even with my lack of experience, I knew the only reason a couple went to the far corner of anywhere was to do some serious necking.

How far did Eli plan to take our pretence? I mean, I've practiced snogging, well, as far as I could with the back my hand and a mirror but did he want us to kiss for real?

Eli turned us around then sat with his back against the wire fence, I joined him.

Shivers, like spiders, ran around every part of my body and it wasn't the cold surface causing it. Eli was fit but I still didn't really know anything about him. Did I want him to kiss me or not? My thoughts spun. I was always so sure about everything but, at that moment, I felt like I'd had an emotion transplant.

Someone had taken sensible, level-headed Jess and replaced her with a hormone-driven girly-girl.

Eli pulled me closer and I felt myself go rigid. What had I gotten myself into?

He lowered his head to mine.

"Relax," he whispered, his warm breath brushing my cheek, "You're too tense; this was your idea, remember?"

How could I forget?

His head came around in front of me, his lips so close to mine not even a hair could get between them. "Put your arms around me," he whispered.

My heart did a strange squeeze, thump, squeeze, thump as I reached up and wrapped my arms around his neck.

"Don't worry, I won't kiss you or do anything you don't want me to do," Eli whispered, his breath brushing my lips.

Kiss me! My emotions urged. *What are you thinking?* My brain argued. My newly split personality was about to go to war when a ball flew across the court and whacked Eli on the side of his head.

"Sh...!" his hand raced to his head. I could see him trying not to let out a string of swear words.

"Sorry!" Liam ran across the court and retrieved the ball.

"That's okay, Mate," Eli said, sounding more normal than he ever had. "Hey, you want me to join you? Make up two on two?"

Liam looked at me and grinned.

"If you're not too busy."

Eli grinned back.

"She'll be all right," he said, using the fence to pull himself up. "Back in a few, Babe."

Babe?

I watched them jog across the court, my stomach a complete mess. He'd brushed me off like an annoying fly. I mean, I know it's the mission and all, but it still hurt.

Is this how he treats his girlfriends? Has he got a real girlfriend?

That was something I hadn't considered before. I sat and scowled, watching the four of them play, wondering whether it made any difference. So, what was I supposed to do while Eli 'bonded' with Liam? One thing I wasn't going to do was sit there and do nothing!

Fair-haired Kian sat in the next corner, playing an imaginary game with a footballer doll in each hand.

I pulled myself up, plastered a smile on my face and walked up to the kid.

"Who's winning?"

Kian shrugged. He was still in school uniform with grey trousers and a blue jumper labelled 'Highwoods Academy', the collar of a red polo shirt showed around his neck.

"Can I play?"

Kian looked up with big brown eyes and my heart went all soft. He was *so* cute! I couldn't help the genuine smile spreading across my face, as I lowered myself down beside him. "You'll have to help me though; I don't know much about football."

"Girls are rubbish at football."

Only four years old and already sexist. Really? I pity his future girlfriends.

A big hand reached inside my chest and squeezed my heart. What was I thinking? If me and Eli fail there won't be any girlfriends, he won't even have a future. In just a few months he'll disappear and never be seen again.

The back of my eyes stung; I wanted to pick him up and take him home with me to keep him safe. I couldn't believe this kid's life was in our hands.

Forcing a smile back on my face, I said. "Some are, some aren't. What're your players' names?" I knew the figures were miniatures of real players but my knowledge of football was only fractionally better than by my knowledge of nuclear physics.

Kian shrugged again.

"So, can I play?"

He frowned then held out the player with a red kit. I took it.

"Thanks. Now where's my goal?"

"Here," Kian said, pointing towards his left elbow. "You'll not score though, your player's rubbish. Mine's the best."

"Oh," I said, raising my eyebrows, "We'll have to see about that, won't we?"

Kian smiled at last, his eyes brightening.

"I'm going to win you!"

"We'll see. Who's blowing the whistle?"

I spent the next fifteen minutes kicking an invisible football across Kian's knees with my footballer doll. Of course, I lost. There's an unwritten law that if you're playing with a young kid, you have to lose.

"See, I won you!!" he declared, his face bright and triumphant. "I told you girls are rubbish at football."

"Yes, you did." I held out my hand. "Come on, let's go see my boyfriend, we might be able to play basketball with them."

Kian's bright smile vanished like the sun behind a cloud. He stuffed his hands into his pockets, frowning.

"Liam won't let me play," he said, his bottom lip sticking out in a sulk.

The basketball pounded on the court as I heard Eli's breathless voice.

"Why don't you like him around?"

"He just gets in the way." Liam's voice was gruff.

"If I had a kid brother, I'd have him around. Girl's love little kids." He paused. "You know what I mean?"

Eli nodded in my direction.

"Not when they're always around. He's a real pain in the …"

I didn't need to hear anymore, neither did Kian. He'd shrunk back into himself, his legs drawn up and head on his knees. Poor kid.

"Hey! How about we go for a walk then? I don't know Mexborough very well, maybe you could show me?"

Kian looked up, his eyes sad.

"I'm not allowed to go nowhere without Liam."

"Well, let's go ask Liam, shall we?" I stood and held out my hand again.

Kian's smile returned as he took my hand, allowing me to pull him to his feet. Still holding hands, we walked across to the boys. Eli bounced the ball, feet slightly apart, ready to dodge Liam. Eli's body looked slim and agile as he twisted and turned before releasing the ball.

"Hey, can I take Kian for a walk?" I called out.

The ball slammed into the ring and whooshed through the net.

"No," Liam snapped, leaving the ball to bounce freely to the court.

"Why not? You're not doing anything with him."

"So? What's it to you?" Liam scowled at the kid. "Kian, go on back down there!" He nodded towards the corner. "What have I told you about talking to strangers?"

Kian looked up at me, his eyes pools of misery, then dropped my hand and shuffled back over to the corner, his head hanging.

I rounded on his older brother, my eyes sparking.

"Call yourself a brother? He's a great kid. You can't keep ignoring him. Why don't you play with him?"

Liam's face darkened.

"It's nowt to do wi' you. Butt out."

"No, I won't! You've got to watch a young kid like that! You never know what …"

My left arm was suddenly yanked so hard I thought it'd leave its socket.

"We've got to go." Eli's voice was urgent. "Sorry, Mate. See you around."

"Get off me!" I yelled, pulling against Eli. "This jerk doesn't know what a great brother he's got. That poor kid's bored stupid over there, he needs attention; he could just wander off!"

"Now, Jess!" Eli glared at me, pulling harder, and I suddenly realised, another minute and I would have spilled it all. I was so angry; I would have told him the future.

I stopped resisting and let Eli lead me away.

"What were you thinking?" He demanded as we left the park. "We were supposed to befriend him, not lecture him. And you were about to tell him everything, weren't you? I could see it in your face."

"But Kian's so cute." I sounded pathetic, even to me. "I couldn't help it. I can't stand the thought of something happening to him. I know I shouldn't have lost it like that but I didn't tell him the future."

"No, but you came close and we might not be able to stop it now." Eli's voice was cold. "Winding him up like that. You could have just blown the whole mission."

***

CHAPTER TWELVE - REGRETS

"If I did, you know, spoil the mission," I said, as we stood waiting for the return bus. "Could they send somebody else?"

Eli shook his head, his lips tight. After telling me off, he hadn't said another word.

"Why not?"

He turned to me, his eyes so accusing I couldn't bear it. Dropping my head, I watched his feet, firm and unmoving in front of me.

"Like I said, the agency's small, there aren't many teams in this area and they'll have their own assignments."

"They can do it with time travel."

"Look, there might be a chance, I don't know; this has never happened on one of my assignments before."

"You said you failed once."

"Not by shouting at the person I was supposed to help." Eli looked away.

I followed his gaze, saw the bus and stuck out my arm. Eli instantly knocked it down.

"Hey!"

"Not this bus," he said, tersely.

"But it's ours."

"It's going to the right place but it's not the one we're meant to catch. We were supposed to be here longer; the time switch is planned for the next bus."

The driver slowed as he drew close then sped up when Eli shook his head.

"What time switch? You said we were on the same day."

"We are but if the time isn't adjusted for you, on the way back, you'll arrive ninety minutes after you set out and you'll have to explain where you've been all that time."

"Me? What about you?"

"My time is adjusted on my bus ride, once I leave you."

"So, when they do the switch …"

"We arrive back on the bus nearest the time just after we set off; that way we don't risk bumping into our earlier selves and there's only a bit of difference in time."

"Oh, okay."

Yep, actually understood that – for a change.

Eli didn't speak at all on the journey back and only gave a brief nod as he turned to go.

"When will we find out about the mission?" I asked.

Eli shrugged. "It'll be Monday now."

"What? Why Monday? How can they expect me to wait all weekend?"

"That's my next scheduled meet. They didn't expect anything to go wrong. We were only supposed to start getting to know them today."

Picking up the accusation in his voice my eyes burned and I blinked hard.

"See you at the end of lunch break, Monday." With that, he turned and walked away, his hands deep in his hoodie pockets. He didn't look back.

My heart felt hard and cold. What if all the bad things still happened and it was all my fault? Kian's wide-eyed face crept into my mind and I couldn't hold back the tears. Right there, in the middle of the street, I bawled, attracting curious stares from two old ladies at the bus stop. This was too much responsibility. It was one thing advising my friends on everyday issues but this was completely different, people's lives were in my hands. Just one mistake and I could have condemned them to a terrible future. Part of my brain told me that was going to be their future anyway, we were only trying to change it for the better, but Kian's little face said otherwise. I mean, what happens to that little boy? Does somebody snatch him and raise him as their own child or do they hurt him?

An agonised groan erupted from my mouth before I could stop it. That couldn't happen, it just couldn't. With blurred vision I checked for traffic and crossed the road. Fishing out a tissue, I dried my face before heading home.

This was going to be the longest weekend, ever.

***

I spent most of my time cross-legged on my 'Princess duvet', (don't laugh – my nan bought it for me last Christmas and I couldn't be cruel and tell her I was, like, eight years too old for it). I could have gone shopping with my friends but I couldn't find any enthusiasm; instead I stared at my blank TV, worrying.

My friends' texts became more concerned as the weekend went on. I refused to meet them and sent only one- or two-word replies, if I bothered to reply at all. Even Mum was worried and by Sunday evening she'd had enough.

"Jessica Hardwick, what's going on with you?" she asked, invading my room, her pink flip-flop slippers slapping against her heels. "You've closeted yourself away like a frightened rabbit all weekend. Are you in trouble?"

Not me but Kian is.

"No, Mum, I'm okay."

"You don't look okay." Mum came over and slapped her hand on my forehead. "You're not hot." She sat on the edge of my bed, her brown eyes trying to read my thoughts. "Is it those girls again?"

"No, Mum, it's just a bit of boy trouble." Well it was, sort-of.

Mum nodded knowingly. "Have you broken up with that boy Queenie's been telling me about?"

"Queenie told you about Eli?"

I don't believe it; my friends have talked to my mum behind my back?

"Now, don't you go getting all upset with them, they're just worried about you."

"But they rang you?"

"No, actually, I rang them."

"Mum!"

"Well, you've been tired and moody ever since those girls beat you up at school and I wanted to make sure you're okay."

"So, you talked to them instead of me?"

Mum gave me her wide-eyed, innocent look.

"Well, it's not like you were ever going to tell me what's going on. You're a teenager Jess, I know that can be tough …"

You don't know the half of it.

"… So, I wanted to know what was going on. Queenie says there's this new boy, very good looking by all accounts." She gave me a knowing nod, her curls bouncing.

"Mu-um!"

"Has he broken up with you? Because if he has, I know how rough that can be, I've been there. There was this one boy, Justin, he had the most gorgeous …"

This sounds like a long story.

"Yeah, Mum, we had an argument, we might have broken up. I'm going to meet him on Monday and try to sort it out."

Mum smiled and tapped her hand on mine.

"That's the spirit, Jess. If you like him, fight for him." Then she frowned. "But don't go chasing after him if he's no good …"

"Oh, he's good, Mum." *At least, I think he is.*

"He's not trying to make you do anything you don't want to, is he? Do we need to have a talk?"

"Mu-u-um! No, we don't need to have a talk. We're just friends, really, but we had an argument. I'll be okay."

"Okay, well, if you need to talk you know where I am."

Well, yeah, I should, we've lived in the same house since I was born.

"Okay, Mum, and thanks." I guess she was only trying to help, she wasn't to know about all the other stuff going on between me and Eli.

"Well, don't let him put you down. You're special and he's an idiot if he let's you go."

"Yeah, mum."

Okay, enough already!

Finally satisfied, Mum left me alone while I tried to decide whether I had, or wanted, a future with the Time Agency.

***

By the time Monday arrived, I felt like a robot with its positronic brain switched off. I'd overloaded; too much thinking and WAY too little sleeping.

My legs took me to each class that morning but don't ask me what was taught. Even an earthquake wouldn't have stirred me. I just stared ahead and wrote things down when everybody else did. Thankfully, the teachers didn't call on me for anything or, at least, if they did, I didn't notice.

I told my friends the same as Mum and re-assured them I'd work things out with Eli. Of course, they were even more convinced we were a couple and I didn't have the energy to correct them, they wouldn't believe me anyway. I did, however, tell them not to say a word to Lisa.

Dinnertime came and there didn't seem any point in my going to the café, there was no way I could eat anything; I hadn't even bothered preparing a packed lunch. Instead, I walked outside and let the fresh air revitalize my frazzled mind. Crossing the tarmac, I reached the gates and peered out.

At the sight of long, blonde hair I dodged back and let the angle of the metal fence give me cover. Leaning out, just enough to see Lisa's back, I watched Eli's hands reaching out, like he was pleading or asking why. I didn't need to hear anything to know it wasn't going well.

Finally, Lisa turned in my direction. I gasped and dodged behind the CLC building. Lisa's heels tapped out her approach and stopped when they reached my hiding place. She turned and stared right at me.

"Ear-wigging were we, Jess?" she said, a grin splitting her face and her eyes sparkling. "So, you *are* working with Eli; you shouldn't have lied to me. Big mistake, one you'll pay for. Bet you fancy him, as well. Just a pity you messed up, big time. Poor little Kian: lost forever and poor Liam: dead so young." She sighed. "What a shame they didn't pick someone better for the job."

Her every word stabbed my heart like an icy spear and I stood, frozen, as she turned and walked away.

When she disappeared around the corner of the school block, the ice melted and I began to burn inside from worry and guilt. I turned and ran out of the gates to Eli.

He leaned against the railings with his head down and hands in his hoodie pockets.

I was desperate to ask what she'd said but, when I reached him, I couldn't speak. I just stood there, waiting.

It seemed like forever before he eventually spoke.

"We're off the case."

I stepped back as though he'd hit me.

"Before she even said anything, I explained what happened and that you never actually revealed the future but Lisa said it didn't matter, by annoying him and saying what you did, the damage was done."

"But, what about Kian?" I asked, my voice no more than a whisper.

Eli lifted his head. "Everything happens the way it would've happened before our visit. Kian disappears, Liam dies young and Ashley ends up in prison," he spat out each word, as though they were poison, his eyes fixed on mine.

"And it's my fault," I said.

I'll give him some credit he didn't say, 'yes it is'. He didn't need to, his eyes said it all.

"Isn't there anything we can do?"

Eli shook his head. "I asked Lisa if I could go on alone; she said she'd ask."

My eyes burned. I'd failed, he hadn't, and now he didn't want to work with me any more but, another part of me was hopeful, if he could still help Kian it wouldn't be so bad.

"Do you think they'll let you?"

"I don't know. I'm sorry for not talking yesterday."

"You were angry, I understand."

"No, it wasn't that, well, yes I was angry but I was more disappointed. I've already failed one mission, it's hard to take." He stared off over my shoulder. "I can't face failing another."

"I'm sorry, it's my fault."

"It's my fault too," he said, "Until Emma's mission I've been with a more experienced partner. They've been training me. Zac helped with everything as well, giving guidance. Then just when I got an inexperienced partner, I got a new go-between, as well. Lisa was no help at all. I guess they expect me to know what I'm doing by now but I didn't keep you under control and I let it get out of hand."

"Keep me under control? I'm not a dog, you know? I know I did wrong but I didn't think what happened was that bad. Why would it do any harm for us to go back? I mean, things are no worse than they were before we went so why can't we still try to make things better?"

Eli sighed. "I argued that point with Lisa but she says it's the Watchers' decision and there's no questioning them. We just have to accept what they say."

"Why? What makes them all-knowing? Well, I don't care what they say. I'm going back. Liam's in the present day so I can just go. I don't need the Watchers. It couldn't do any harm, could it?"

"It's your present day, not mine, so I couldn't go with you. I can't even meet you without the Watchers' help. The thing is, if you go against them on this they might not give you another mission and there're loads of others who need you. Without the Watchers you won't even know about them." He gazed at me, his eyes so intense, like he was desperate to tell me something but couldn't, in the end, he just shook his head. "You can't quit, Jess. Please."

What's going on in your head?

I watched him; his expression so serious. This was more than just the mission or even him fancying me, if he did. There was something much deeper, like, he needed me. But why would he need me so badly?

For my part, I couldn't imagine not seeing him again and, although it's stressful, I'd miss the missions. Helping others is so special; it feels good to make a difference in someone's life. But then, on the other hand, did I want to continue with something where one small mistake could be so devastating? I mean, I'm just a teenager and a long way from perfect.

"So, what happens now?" I asked.

"We've got another mission. Or should I say, you have. It's a test. If you fail this one then your probation period ends and you're out."

"I'm on probation? I didn't know that."

"We all are, at first. You really need to pull this one off."

"So, what's the mission?"

I didn't really want to know. I wanted to help Kian but I couldn't help anyone if I got kicked out. Although, I hadn't given up on the idea of going on my own, maybe apologising to Liam and seeing if I could still do some good. So long as I stayed away from CCTV and kept no record of my visits they wouldn't know, would they? I mean, Lisa's been pulling it off for years.

"It's to do with your friend, Leah."

"Leah?" I'm ashamed to say that all thoughts of Kian vanished in an instant and were replaced with Leah. How could something bad happen to quiet, shy Leah? "It's not that dirt bag boyfriend of hers, is it? She doesn't go and sleep with him, does she?"

Eli shook his head.

"No, she doesn't, and that's the problem."

"What?" This didn't make any sense.

"He dumps her because she won't sleep with him and she's so upset she takes some pills." He paused. "Jess, Leah dies."

"No!"

My knees felt like they wouldn't hold me up anymore and I grabbed for the railings. Not again, this couldn't happen again. Images of my older sister, Jen, stung my mind. Happy, full of life and now gone.

"But I'm the one who told her not to sleep with him." My words were no more than a whisper; I had no breath for more.

"For all the right reasons."

"I can't believe it turns out that way." I still held onto the railings, shaking my head. "She wouldn't take pills, it doesn't sound like her, at all." But then, I'd never have believed Jen could either.

Eli didn't say anything he just watched me. He was really good at just watching.

"What am I supposed to do?" My voice sounded flat and empty, just like my heart, "Can I stop her taking the pills?"

"Lisa says she'll have to sleep with him."

"What? No way! He's a sleaze-bag and a creep. It can't be best for her to sleep with him! He'll probably dump her as soon as it's over then she'll be worse than ever. She'll end it, like…"

Pressure built up behind my eyes. I'd solve any problem, do any mission but not this. I shook my head.

"I can't do it." My voice quivered and my chest felt like it was in a car crusher.

"Jess? What's the matter?"

"My sister, Jen…"

"You've never told me you have a sister called Jen."

"I've never told you about any of my family."

"Oh, er, yeah, of course."

I peered at him, he sounded like he'd just said something wrong but what could be wrong about that? Unless the Watchers had told him about my family and he wasn't supposed to let on that he knew. But if they'd told him about Abby and Jimmy then they'd have told him about Jen, as well, wouldn't they?

"Do you want to tell me about her?"

"Jen had a sleaze-bag boyfriend like Jake. He kept pestering her to sleep with him, she was crazy about him, so she did. The next day he dumped her, told everyone she was easy and had slept with all his friends. They all backed him up. Like me, she blushed really easily and everything they said made her face bright red so everyone believed them. People are always so quick to believe gossip. They sent her messages on Facebook calling her a … well, you know. Everyone stared. Even some of her 'so-called' friends doubted her and went along with the crowd. Horrible things were written on her locker and on her school bag after Phys. Ed. She couldn't take it. She took mum's sleeping pills. It was three years ago. She would have been eighteen next month."

"She died?" Eli looked as though I'd just told him the world would end tomorrow. "I'm so sorry, Jess."

Eli put his hand on my arm but I didn't feel any better. He wore that sympathetic look that everyone gets when they hear about it. I hate that and didn't want to see it on his face.

"It wasn't your fault, you know."

I couldn't even nod in agreement.

"It wasn't," he insisted, "It was the boy who pushed her into sex before she was ready and it was the kids at school who shouldn't have judged – half of them were probably doing the same thing – but everyone loves a scandal and to have someone to gossip about. I'm so sorry it was your sister."

"They shouldn't do that to anyone." The emptiness and frustration I'd felt for years seeped up to the service again. It made me want to hit every one of those who hurt my sister. My fists clenched and I blinked quickly, trying to drive back the tears.

"No, they shouldn't. Their words and actions, online and in person is what caused her to … take her own life, they caused it, not you."

"But I still feel guilty for not seeing how really bad she felt. I knew she was sad, but I didn't know it was that bad. I wonder if I'd told her not to sleep with him, said something different to her afterwards or stayed in her room that night so she couldn't take the pills, would she still be alive?"

"Jess, you were eleven years old."

"It doesn't matter."

"You couldn't have known what she was going to do."

"I know, but it doesn't help."

"I guess not." Eli didn't seem to know what else to say, he stuck his hands in his pockets and stared away, down the road.

"That's why you try to help people, isn't it?" he said, eventually. "Because of your sister."

I nodded. Wiping my moist eyes, I took a deep breath and looked up at him.

"Look, I'll talk to Leah this afternoon and see how it goes, okay? But I'm making no promises. I like Leah and sleeping with that sleaze is the worst thing she could do." I paused, a thought springing into my mind. "Lisa obviously knows I work with you now. The Watchers must have told her; maybe to explain why the mission with Kian and Liam had to end. So, what if she's just saying this to get at me?"

Eli frowned. "She wouldn't dare, would she?"

"She'd do anything to hurt me and she probably knows about Jen. Jen used to come to this school; Lisa would have been here when it all happened."

"But, if Lisa made all this up, just to hurt you, her job with the agency would be over. Does she hate you that much?"

I shrugged. "Maybe."

"Then I don't know what to say. You know Leah better than me. It's up to you."

"No pressure then."

Eli walked with me to the gates and stopped beside the CLC building.

"Good luck."

I grimaced and continued on into school. What was I supposed to do now? If I made the wrong decision I would ruin, or maybe even end, Leah's life. A glance at my watch told me there were only five minutes before the bell and no time to talk to her now. I'd have to wait. I needed time to think, anyway.

Maths was the first lesson. We were doing algebra, normally one of my strengths but today it just passed by me like a ghost. I stared at the list of equations in the text book and couldn't work out a thing. I didn't care what x was in '$x = A / (C - B)$ where $A = 9$, $B = -2$ and $C = 7$'.

Instead, my mind flitted between images of Leah and Jen while I tried to work out a different way to save her.

"Jess Hardwick, have you attempted any of these problems yet?" Mrs Quinn's voice penetrated my thoughts.

"Er, yes, er, no, Miss."

"Bring your book here!"

I picked up my exercise book, with its condemning blank page, and walked slowly to the front, aware that every eye in the room was watching me.

"Everyone else, back to work!" Every head, in the four rows of desks, dropped back to their books.

"What's going on, Jessica?" she asked, holding the exercise book like a piece of evidence. "Why haven't you done any work?"

"Sorry, Miss."

"Do you have an explanation?"

"No, Miss." I mean, what could I say? 'I can't concentrate, Miss, because I'm trying to decide whether to tell my friend to have sex with a sleaze so she doesn't top herself?' Yeah, right.

Mrs Quinn took a deep breath, her jaw tight, lips pursed. She lowered her voice.

"Is this anything to do with Lisa?"

The shock must have shown on my face, I mean, I'm no poker player, I can't hide my feelings very well. I didn't know what to say. It was everything to do with Lisa but not in the way she thought.

"Ah, I see that it is." Mrs Quinn frowned. "It seems I need to have words with that young lady."

My breathing stopped.

"No, Miss, don't, please," I pleaded, equally quietly. "I'll sort it, Miss. And I'll do all those equations by the end of the lesson."

The bell rang and my shoulders sagged.

An expectant pause filled the room, all pens poised, faces focused on the teacher.

"Your homework is to do the questions on page 50. You are dismissed."

The room instantly erupted with the thunder of chairs scraping and the rustle of pens and paper being scooped up and pushed unceremoniously into bags.

"I'll do them tonight, Miss, as homework," I said, above the racket. "I promise."

"As well as page 50."

"Yes, Miss."

"Very well, but pay attention in class from now on." I felt my muscles relax. "I'll be keeping a close eye on you and Miss Smith and will intervene at any further sign of trouble, do you understand?"

"Yes, Miss," I said, quickly.

Mrs Quinn fixed me with her icy-blue gaze for several seconds while I tried to figure out whether I was supposed to stay or go.

"You may go," she said, at last, so I grabbed by bag and fled, exercise book in hand.

The last thing I needed was Mrs Quinn getting involved, that would *so* not help anything, although it was good to know she was on my side.

Getting through the rest of the afternoon was a nightmare; part of me wanted it to go faster so that I could try to save Leah and the other half wanted it never to end because I had no idea what to say to her. I wanted to tell her to stay away from him but if Lisa was telling the truth I'd be hurting her. If I told her to go with him and Lisa was lying that would be just as bad. If I didn't do either and just told her she's worth more than him, and should never hurt herself because of him, she could get angry with me and turn against me in favour of Jake. Then she wouldn't come to me when Jake hurt her and, knowing him, no matter what choices Leah made, he would eventually hurt her.

    It was an impossible decision and, when school finally ended, I pulled myself out of my chair, after English, headed into the corridor and bumped straight into Lisa.

    "Going to talk to your little friend now?" I cringed as she whispered in my ear. "Don't mess up again or you'll have one less friend tomorrow."

    "You're enjoying this, aren't you?" I spat, turning to glare at her. "Why you were ever picked to be a go-between, I'll never know."

    For an instant something flashed in her eyes, was it anger or hurt? I couldn't tell, it was gone so fast.

    "Hush now, Jess," Lisa crooned. "We can't have you spouting off and letting others know about the Agency. That's sure to get your probation terminated; not to mention making everyone at school think you're a head case for talking about time travel."

    "You mentioned time travel not me and, right now, I don't care anyway." That was a lie, of course, but I wouldn't let Lisa think she could intimidate me.

    "Yeah, sure you don't. Just make sure you do your mission."

    "But who's the mission from, the Watchers or you?"

"That's one you'll have to work out for yourself but be careful, Leah's life depends on you making the right choice."

I wanted to wipe the grin off Lisa's face as she turned and strode away. She was soon swallowed up by the tide of uniforms heading for the doors; I wished it was a shark that had swallowed her. I followed more slowly, knowing my friends would wait to say goodbye before heading home in different directions.

Queenie and Leah were already in the car park waiting near the small CLC building. Chad stood with them, looking bored. Boy-jerk Jake was nowhere to be seen.

"Hiya!" I said, faking cheerfulness. "How's things?"

"Okay," they replied in triplicate.

"So, Leah, where's boy-je …, erm, where's Jake?"

"He's gonna be a bit late. He got in trouble with Mr Henshaw this morning and has to go back and see him."

"Are you gonna wait for him?"

Leah looked defensive, "Yeah, 'course. He'll not be long."

"Oh, okay. I'll wait with you."

I could've told Leah I was an alien and she wouldn't have looked more surprised.

"Well, we're going," Queenie said. "I'll see you later."

"Later?" I looked at her, totally blank.

"Guitar practise, seven o'clock, like every Monday?" Queenie spoke slowly as though she was talking to a foreigner.

"Oh, yeah."

"You know, Jess, sometimes I think when God issued brains, you didn't even join the queue."

"Gee thanks, Queenie."

Queenie just shrugged, linked arms with Chad and led him away.

I waited until they were out of earshot before speaking.

"So, Leah, how's it going with Jake?"

"It's good."

"That's good." Even I could hear the lack of conviction in my voice.

"I'm not breaking up with him, Jess."

I looked at my friend, surprised.

"I wasn't going to tell you to." *But I wish you would.*

"But you want me to."

Did she just read my mind?

"Look, I care about you and don't like him pressuring you to sleep with him."

"But it's my choice, you said so."

"And I still say it." *Here goes.* "But I don't like him and I think he's no good for you." Leah opened her mouth to protest but I kept talking. "But it is your choice and if you really feel you want to do it then it's up to you."

"Really?" Leah squinted at me and chewed her thumb nail. "I love him, Jess. He's my first real boyfriend and I don't want to lose him, so I was thinking about it."

Someone tied a knot around my heart and pulled tight. I remembered Jen saying the same thing.

"It's a big decision and you have to be sure he's worth it."

"He is worth it!" Leah snapped then her face and voice softened. "I don't want to lose him, Jess."

"Look, Leah, this is no-one's choice except yours, not even Jake's. He decides for his body and you decide for yours but, whatever you do, remember you're still young, there'll be other boys or men. Your life matters; don't let him ruin it."

"I'm not going to end up like Jen."

Familiar pain skewered my heart and Leah must have realised because she blushed and spoke quickly.

"I'm sorry, Jess, I shouldn't have said that."

"It's okay. It's just that I care about you and don't want you to be hurt."

"I know but I'm okay and he's not going to ruin my life. I know you care but I wish you weren't always so down on him. If you were a true friend you'd support me, no matter what."

If I were a true friend? That's so not fair; I've always been there for her.

I swallowed down the hurt before opening my mouth. "I do support you. I just want you to make the right choice for you."

"Then trust me to make it."

"I do."

"It doesn't sound like it." Leah stood. "I'm going to meet Jake."

She walked away from me without looking back. I watched her go, wondering whether I'd made things better or worse. She'd never said so much or so firmly before. Had I pushed her towards him? Was that what I was supposed to do? Would she still be alive tomorrow?

I walked towards the gates, making plans.

I'd give her time to meet Jake then go to her house. She might not reply to texts but she couldn't ignore someone at her door. Even if she did, her mother wouldn't. Her mother would let me in.

Whatever happened, I would do my best to save Leah and if the agency didn't like my interfering directly and sacked me then so be it.

***

CHAPTER THIRTEEN – PROBLEMS

"How're you doing, Jess?"

"Aargh!" Jumping, I spun around to the source of the voice, just centimetres from my left ear. "Where'd you come from? You weren't there a second ago."

Eli gave me a lazy grin, his eyebrows raised.

"Oh yeah, time travel but, if you can just materialise like that, how come when we're together we always have to catch a bus?"

Eli shrugged. "I hadn't gone anywhere I just moved time not place. The bus takes us where we're going and makes it less likely that we're seen appearing and disappearing. I don't know why they've brought me back again; I was just about to go home. It's weird. I watched you walk away then felt the dizziness of the time shift and you were right in front of me again; it's never happened like that before. What day is this?"

"It's the same day as before but after school. I've just spoken to Leah."

"How'd it go?"

"Rotten. I wouldn't tell her to sleep with him but I didn't tell her not to, either. The more I said the more she sided with him. I think I might have pushed her towards him."

"Well, that's what you were supposed to do."

"That's what Lisa said I was supposed to do but is it true? I thought we were supposed to let them make their own choices?"

"We are but we steer people the right way."

"But is this the right way?"

"I don't know but you know Lisa and Leah better than me. Anyway, you didn't make the decision for her you just pointed her in the right direction."

"I don't even know the right direction. I don't trust Lisa or Jake."

"Eli!" The manly voice came from outside the gates. Turning, I saw a young man with the wildest blond hair I'd ever seen. It stuck out in all directions but really suited his slim face. He wore hipster black jeans with neon green trainers and a black polo neck jumper with fluorescent stripes. I blinked a couple of times but he was still there and his colour scheme hadn't changed.

"Zac?"

I looked at Eli and back to the glowing boy, well, I think he was a boy rather than a man. His voice was deep but his face only looked to be about eighteen or nineteen.

"That's Zac?"

Eli nodded.

"He dresses a bit …"

"Flamboyantly?"

"Yeah."

"Apparently, all men dress like that when he comes from. It's the women who wear dull clothes in the future and the men dress to impress."

"How do you know?"

Eli grinned. "I asked him."

"And he told you?"

"Yep." He walked over to Zac and I followed, wondering why Eli got answers about the future and I never did.

Zac glanced at me then focussed on Eli.

"We've got problems," he began.

"What kind of problems? Why are you making contact instead of Lisa?"

"There's been a time disturbance, a change that wasn't meant to happen."

Zac glanced at me again.

"What? Are you saying it's my fault, this disturbance? How can it be? I've only done what I was told. Well, nearly."

"Whatever you said to your friend Leah altered history. What did you do that you wouldn't normally do?"

"I talked to her about sleeping with Jake but I've done that before. I didn't tell her to do it, I couldn't. I said it was her choice but sort-of-said, he wasn't worth it. Normally, I'd tell her to wait until she was ready. This time, I was less against it than usual because I was supposed to get her to do it for the mission but I might have come across as more against Jake. I think I upset her."

"What mission? You don't have a mission that involves Leah."

"But Lisa …" I stopped. "Lisa set me up, didn't she? I was right. She wants to hurt me by making me hurt Leah; the vindictive, scheming, evil witch. Wait 'till I get my hands on her!"

My hands clenched tight but if Lisa had been there they'd have been wrapped around her scrawny neck.

"Lisa? What does she have to do with this?"

"She told us Leah had to sleep with Jake or he'll dump her and she'll commit suicide." Eli explained.

Zac nodded. "That explains the note, to some extent."

"What note?" I asked.

"The one left by Leah. She sleeps with Jake today. Tomorrow he tells the school and says she 'performed' badly. He dumps her. Unable to take the humiliation, as well as having lost her first love, she runs away. She leaves a note for her parents in which she also says sorry to you, Jess. She says that you told her it was okay to sleep with Jake but then trashed him. She decided to prove you wrong about him but you were right all along. We don't know exactly what happens but the indications are that she lives on the streets for a while before her body is found in ten months time, murdered."

My hand clamped around my mouth and tears filled my eyes.

No, she can't die, she just can't!

My tears spilled as Zac continued.

"Her family line has vanished. None of her family had a major influence from now until the Watchers' generation but it's enough to cause a time disruption. They had to boost the power to send Eli and me back as some minor time waves are still rippling through."

"What do you mean, 'her family didn't have a major influence'? How can you talk like that? People are dead because of me! Leah's dead because of me! I failed her just like I failed Jen!" My throat felt so tight I could hardly breathe. "It can't happen again, it just can't!"

"It hasn't yet." Eli's voice was soft.

"What?" I sniffed and rubbed my nose with my sleeve.

"Leah isn't dead yet, you have time."

"Not much, if you want to stop the inciting incident." Zac said, checking his watch.

"The what?"

Zac rolled his eyes, "Them having sex. It seems Jake bragged about it being after school with teachers still around."

"That's now! She's meeting him now! I've got to go!"

"Jess, wait." Zac grabbed my arm. "One thing you need to know. The agency would never advise a teenager to sleep with someone, especially if they don't really want to. If Lisa has had anything to do with this, we'll investigate."

"Yeah, whatever." I shook my arm free. At that moment, I didn't care about Lisa or the Agency or time disturbances, I only cared about Leah. I had to find her but where would Jake have taken her?

I raced around the main building to the bottom yard. She wasn't there. Bounding down the steps, I raced towards the tennis courts but when I arrived, panting, I found them empty too.

Leah, where are you?

Retracing my steps, I ran around the science block, my feet making a dull splat, splat on the tarmac.

The few staff cars had gone and on the small stretch of grass, backing onto the cemetery, Leah lay on her back with Jake propped up on his left arm beside her. He was stroking her hair and talking softly but I was too far away to make out his words. Leah just lay stiff and still, her head tilted towards him. Was I too late?

When I'd almost reached them, Jake saw me and a deep frown creased his forehead.

"What're you doing here? Come to perv?"

Leah's head turned, her eyes widening when she saw me.

"Jess?"

"Can I have a word, Leah?"

"Now's not a good time," Jake said, a leer crossing his lips, "We're a bit busy over here."

"It might be important," Leah said; her voice barely more than a whisper.

"Yes, it is. REAL important," I said.

"Yeah, and what we're doing is real important, isn't it, Babe?" The look he gave Leah told her not to disagree.

Leah looked from me to him and back but said nothing.

"Sorry to interrupt your 'important' thing, Jake, but this is more important. Leah, I need to talk to you, now!"

"More important, is it?" Jake barked. "Listen to you, Miss High and Mighty. Well I call the shots around here and Leah stays with me. You hear me?"

"I'd better see what she wants." Leah sounded like an apologetic child as she sat up.

Jake immediately pushed her back down.

"You're staying put! You've kept me waiting forever and now you've agreed. You're not backing out now!"

"You leave her alone!" I marched forwards; my jaw so tight my teeth felt like they were being crushed. "Leah can decide what she wants for herself."

"Get out of here, Hardwick, or you'll be sorry!" Jake's eyes were dark and full of menace. All moisture left my mouth. He was way bigger than me and one of the toughest lads in school. If he wanted, he could cause me a whole world of pain.

"It's okay, Jess." Leah's voice sounded small. "I'll erm, I'll stay here with Jake; you go on now, it's okay."

The wobble in her voice and her pale face told me it was *so* not okay.

"I'm sorry Leah. I was too pushy. If you chose this because of me then don't do it but if it's what you really want then I'll leave."

And I'll stick to your side like superglue tomorrow so you can't run away.

I wanted to drag her away but my limited mission experience reminded me Leah had to make the decision herself. If I interfered forcibly, she could fall out with me and stay with him anyway; then when it went wrong, she wouldn't feel she could come to me for help. She had to know I was there for her, no matter what. I watched her inner debate, confusion written all over her frowning face. The wait was killing me. I couldn't fail her like I'd failed Jen.

"It is what she wants, so get lost," Jake ordered, his strong paw pressed against her shoulder.

"Is it, Leah?" I asked.

"I want to get up now, Jake," she said quietly, her voice surprisingly calm.

"Well, you don't always get what you want, do you? You made me a promise and you're gonna deliver. Stay and watch if you want!" He grinned at me then reached down and lifted Leah's skirt.

"Get off me, Jake!" Leah yelled, trying to push his hand away but he kept it firmly against her thigh, sliding it upwards.

"Oh no, you don't!" I rushed forwards and launched myself at him, hitting his right side and rolling him over. My momentum took me with him and we rolled, together. We came to rest with me on my back on the grass and Jake lying face down on top of me.

"You'll pay for that!" he yelled, "You've always got to stick your big nose in where it's not wanted!"

His strong grip squeezed my arms to the bone.

"Ow! Get off me!" I yelled, but he didn't.

Instead, he raised himself up, trapped my arms under his knees then closed his right hand into a fist. Unable to defend myself, I closed my eyes and turned my face away, waiting for the excruciating impact.

But it didn't happen.

"What the …?" At Jake's exclamation I opened my eyes, just a crack, to see Eli, his knuckles white with the strain of holding back Jake's hand.

It was a weirdly positioned arm wrestle and I hardly dared breathe as I waited for the outcome. If Eli lost my face would be the first to know and, given the effort Jake was exerting, there probably wouldn't be much of my face left after impact.

Struggling, I tried to free my arms but, with all Jake's weight on his knees, I stood no chance. All I could do was lie there and hope I still had a face at the end of their battle.

Jake's fist moved up and down as first Eli made progress then Jake.

How the arm wrestle would've turned out I don't know, as both boys suddenly lurched to my right. Jake rolled off me completely while Eli fell flat across my body, his legs flattening my stomach.

I saw Leah fall. She'd pushed them so hard her forward motion kept her going. She landed on Eli's legs which, in turn, dug deep into my stomach.

"Umph!" I hissed as every nano-drop of air pushed out of my body. Bile filled my mouth and, clamping my lips firmly shut, I swallowed hard to keep from being sick.

From the edge of my vision I saw Jake push himself up and stride towards us. Eli was as helpless as me with Leah crushing him. But, at the sight of the advancing Jake, Leah jumped up and faced him.

"Don't even think about it, Jake!" she yelled, her right index finger wagging. "You're a bully, who's only after one thing. Jess is right, I should have seen through you ages ago. Well, it's over, okay? It's over."

"No way is it over!" Jake yelled, his face so red it looked ready to explode. "Nobody makes me look stupid and gets away with it."

"Nobody's made you look stupid except yourself and anyway, look around." Leah spread her arms wide, "There's nobody here to see anything except us and we're not going to say anything, are we, Jess, Eli?"

She looked from me to Eli, her face saying she'd asked a question but it wasn't a multi-choice answer.

"No," I said, reluctantly, as we finally managed to untangle ourselves and sit up. "We'll not say anything."

Jake wavered for a minute, his fists clenched, looking at each of us in turn.

"Okay, I'm going." He poked his finger close to Leah's face as he passed. "But don't think this is over because it isn't. You're all gonna regret this."

He finished with a glare at me and Eli then stomped away.

Leah let out a huge sigh and visibly deflated. "Phew, that was *way* too tense!"

I drew up my legs and wrapped my arms around them.

"It was crazy," I agreed, still visualising his fist near my face; my body still felt cold at the thought of what could have happened.

"But it felt good." Leah looked at me, her eyes sparkling. "Is this what it feels like to stand up for yourself? I've never done it before but it feels fantastic!"

I smiled at her then at Eli. He wasn't smiling, in fact, he looked worried. My smile faded. What was he worried about? We'd succeeded, hadn't we? Even better than we could have expected, so what was the problem? I had no idea but, as soon as Leah left, I was going to find out.

***

CHAPTER FOURTEEN – FALL OUT

Leah stayed another half hour. She needed to talk it all through and I didn't want to stop her,
 even though my insides were twitching like an ants' nest.

When she'd finally had enough, she looked from me to Eli.

"So, are you two an item, or what?"

"No," I said too quickly, feeling flames ignite in my cheeks, again! These days, I spend so much time blushing I must look like the healthiest fourteen-year-old on the planet! Either that or someone with a permanently high temperature.

She looked at Eli, pointedly

"We're just friends," Eli confirmed with his enigmatic smile.

Why do I wish he'd said something else?

Leah sucked her lips.

"Okay, sure, you're just 'friends'." Her fingers did a little quotation around 'friends'. "Real handy you were around though, wasn't it? You're around a lot lately."

"Leah!" I couldn't believe this, she was never this blunt, at least, not around people she didn't really know. "We're interested in the same things, that's all."

"Yeah, I bet you are." Leah grinned then walked away.

I watched her go, my cheeks still burning. Not wanting to look at Eli, I continued to look in the direction she had gone, even though she had already rounded the corner and was out of sight.

"She didn't believe us," I said.

"No kidding? Anyway, it doesn't matter."

"Not to you."

"Would it be so bad for her to think I'm your boyfriend?"

My cheeks could have melted an igloo.

"I guess not, if *you* don't mind," I said, switching my gaze to examine the scuffs on my shoes. Was Eli actually saying he wanted to go out with me or was I reading this wrong? I decided it would be safer to change the subject. "A while ago you looked worried. What's up?"

"Leah asked whether standing up for yourself always felt this good or something like that. Has she ever stood up for herself before?"

"Not that I know of, she's always been a 'yes' person, going along with everyone else. I've been trying to get her out of it for years but until now she's never …" Light dawned and I looked up at Eli. "History's changed again, hasn't it? Leah's future will be different now she's learned to stand up for herself. That's not a bad thing though, is it? She's going to be okay, isn't she?"

"I don't know," Eli shook his head. "We'll have to talk to Zac."

"Will he still be here?"

"I doubt it. They won't be able to keep us both here with the time lines changing, it's amazing they haven't pulled me out, but we can go see."

A quick scan outside school told us Zac had gone.

"So, what do we do now?" I asked.

"We'll have to wait for him to get in touch with me."

"Eli, I can't wait! What if she still dies, I need to know!"

"I don't think she'll die; her future might just be a bit different, that's all."

"Different how?"

"I've no idea but nothing bad, I don't think."

"You don't think! Eli! Is she going to be okay or not?"

"Zac'll get in touch and tell me."

My body felt like a balloon with too much air pumped into it, the pop would be loud, and soon. Didn't Eli, Zac and the Watchers know how important this was? I closed my eyes, wishing there was something I could do.

"In the mean time what do I do about Lisa the Lizard?"

Eli smirked.

"Lizard, hey?"

"It suits her."

"Well, just treat her like any other lizard."

"Yeah, right. I wish she'd shoo off so easily. Will Zac be coming all the time now?"

"Hopefully, he said that after Lisa's interference he'd talk to the Watchers. She'll probably be tossed out of the Agency."

"Wow, she'll not like that. She'll really be after me now."

"I hope not."

I looked into his handsome face; he really sounded concerned for me. No boy had ever been bothered about me before, not even my brother.

"I've just had a thought," I said. "I rushed off to keep Leah from sleeping with Jake but I could have just gone back in time and changed what I said. I could just have told her not to do it."

"No, you couldn't."

"Why not?"

"Well, for one thing, she might not have listened and, for another, you don't go back into your own skin."

"Huh?"

Eli frowned. "It's hard to explain but the original 'you' from that moment would still be there so there'd be two of you, which would freak everyone out if they saw you both; or, you'd get to Leah before the original 'you' and, whatever you said, the original 'you' would meet her afterwards and undo it."

"I don't get it."

Eli sighed. "You couldn't be transported back to the exact time of the conversation because there'd then be two of you. You couldn't be transported back to after your conversation because it would be too late, as she'd already gone to meet Jake. If you went earlier whatever you said to her would be undone when the original 'you' met her afterwards. Get it?"

I got it as much as I got nuclear physics but, hey, science wasn't my strong subject. In the end, I just nodded and accepted that I couldn't have done anything any differently.

I walked with Eli as far as Knapton Avenue where I needed to turn off.

"I'll be in touch," he said and continued on to Blythe Avenue and the bus stop.

I guessed that's why he was late coming to rescue Leah; Zac must have been telling him how to time-travel back home again.

I watched Eli go, a longing sigh rising up from my toes. If only I knew him under normal circumstances ... but no, he probably wouldn't look at me twice if it wasn't for the agency.

***

"Why weren't you at guitar practice?" Queenie accused as soon as she saw me, outside the gates, the next morning.

"Oh, er, sorry, I forgot."

"But I only reminded you at the end of school!"

"Yeah, I know. Things came up."

"Like what?"

"Just things." I glanced at Leah, who smiled.

"Lips," Leah said with her head high and back straight.

"Whose lips?" Queenie asked.

"Eli's." Leah's smile twisted mischievously.

"Leah!" I gasped looking around to be sure no one had heard and feeling the familiar flush in my cheeks. "We did not kiss!"

"I know; you're just 'friends'." She did the finger quote again. "But I saw the way you looked at each other."

Again with the looks.

"Maths came up," I said, quickly. "I had a lot of homework." Which was true. "Anyway, Leah, how's things with you?"

"Great," she said, "Never better."

"Don't go changing the subject. Come on, Jess, spill." Tammy's eyes sparkled with curiosity. "You've been holding out on us for too long."

"Nothing to tell," I lied. "We're just friends, like I keep saying." And secret Time Fixers.

"Leah?" Queenie asked.

"Well, they were together after I left yesterday and he's definitely hot, as you've seen. Their body language said they were more than friends."

"What body language?" I asked, unable to stop myself.

"Woah," Tammy whistled, "So Jess's got a boyfriend, at last."

"No, I haven't," I denied, "I know you want to think so, and maybe it might look like it, but I haven't and stop making me sound so desperate."

I have to get Leah on her own and ask about this body language stuff. What am I missing?

"I think you're protesting too much," Queenie said. "You've admitted you like him and who wouldn't? He's scrummy. And remember the rating you gave him? Tammy told me all about it."

"Yeah, I remember," I admitted. "But I only said I liked him to shut you all up."

"Yeah, whatever." Queenie gave a wave of her hand that clearly said she didn't believe me.

Lisa came into sight, walking down the road, and my good feeling sagged, like my sponge cakes in domestic science, but at the same time a fire ignited in my stomach. I wanted to head straight over and tell her exactly what a nasty, stinking, piece of slime she really was but, before I could do anything, the bell rang for registration. I wasn't sure which of us had been saved by the bell, her or me.

All through French, I was aware of Leah sitting beside me. She seemed to be more alert than usual, sitting straighter and answering more questions, or was I just paying more attention? She didn't seem depressed at all, in fact, she seemed happier than she'd been since she started going out with Jake. I chewed my nails, hoping all this was a sign that her future would be better, not worse. I hoped it wasn't an act she was putting on to cover up her real feelings.

As soon as the lunch bell rang, I ran straight out to the street but there was no sign of Eli. I paced up and down for ten minutes, hoping he would appear, but he never showed. In the end, I had to give up or risk missing lunch.

My feet dragged back to the café and I picked up a tray. Joining the end of the queue, I scanned the crowded room to see if my friends were still there.

I soon spotted them but also saw Lisa and co striding, away from the counter, towards the alcove where they were sitting, grazing like naive gazelles. None of them had noticed the pack of lionesses heading their way. My hands tightened on the tray until it bit into my fingers.

Lisa positioned herself behind Tammy as Queenie looked up, her mouth dropping open to reveal half-chewed chips. If I hadn't been so anxious for Tammy I would've been totally revolted.

"You're in my seat." Lisa's voice wasn't loud but I had tuned in enough to hear her. Tables near them hushed as I looked around for the dinner ladies. As usual, Lisa had picked her moment, there was only one at the counter, ahead of me, and she was serving. Should I interrupt and tell her what was happening or just go and help my friends?

Tammy turned to look up at Lisa, indecision clear on her face. Should she move or stay?

I put down my empty tray and left the queue.

As Tammy began to stand, Lisa had her back to me but I could imagine the look of triumph on her face.

"She's not moving!" I said, striding up behind Lisa.

Lisa turned; her face smug.

"Oh, I think she is."

"No. She's not," I said, firmly. "Sit down, Tammy."

Tammy's eyes flicked between me and Lisa, her body frozen half on and half off the stool.

"She's going to move or she'll have to deal with the consequences," Lisa spat, "You too."

I shrugged. "Whatever."

My heart played a fast march and my knees quivered in rhythm. It was taking every bit of my strength to keep the panic from showing on my face.

"I'll deal with them too." Leah rose from her seat on the other side of the table. She stood tall and straight, determination etched on her face from her glaring eyes to her firmly set mouth. "We're all staying, Lisa. We're not moving."

Queenie looked like she was gonna throw up. Everyone nearby was in freeze-frame, like someone had pressed the pause button.

Tammy slowly sank back onto her stool. "I'm not moving."

Lisa just stared. If anger produced smoke it would be puthering from her ears, nose and mouth. There were four of us and four of them, an even match. Lisa didn't like even matches but if she backed down now she'd look weak, others would stand up to her and her vicious reign would end.

She decided to gamble.

"Get her," she ordered.

There was a clatter as her cronies pushed trays away on either side of my friends, put down their own trays then converged on Tammy.

All colour left Tammy's face as she cringed against the table.

My brain raced through the options and settled on the best it could manage.

Grabbing the nearest glass of water, I ordered. "Leave her alone!"

"Or what?" Lisa smirked as her friends grabbed Tammy's arms.

"Or this!" I said and launched the water at her chest.

"Aargh!" she screamed, flapping her arms at her soaking shirt. But she was too late; her shirt was already transparent revealing a white bra, with a lacy pattern, underneath. At least she was wearing a bra, I mean, if she wasn't, I would NOT want to be standing directly in front of her. Eew!

"Pheww!" a few boys whistled. "Nice bra!"

"You are so dead, Jess Hardwick!" she screamed as stifled laughter spread across the room. Only my friends sat in stunned silence, obviously worried about how much fallout from this would land on their heads - literally.

"What's going on over there?" a dinner lady's voice called.

Lisa's jaw clenched, her eyes firing lazer beams.

"You'd better watch your back!" she snarled. "Girls!"

Her friends dropped Tammy like a cold chip and marched out after their soaking leader.

Scattered applause broke out and rippled across the room before the door swung shut.

"Way to go, Jess!"

"About time somebody got her back!"

"Did you see her face?"

Well, if that was a scientific experiment, I could now state it was possible to feel satisfied, proud and absolutely terrified all at the same time. With Lisa out of the room, my adrenaline levels dropped and I knew there would be mega payback.

"You've done it now," said Queenie, her usually brown face, now a shade of grey.

"I was going to move," Tammy said, her voice quivering.

"You did good," said Leah and somehow that worried me even more.

My chest tightened, squeezing around my heart like a fist, as I suddenly wished I'd never heard of the Time Agency or Lisa.

***

CHAPTER FIFTEEN - MISSION

"Hey, look out, lover-boy's waiting."

Leah looked over my shoulder with a knowing smile.

Eli was in his usual position, leaning back against the railings, watching the gates. The hoodie was gone, replaced by a green T-shirt and black tracksuit bottoms. Not a bad look.

"Well?" Leah urged. "Go to lover-boy."

"He's not lover-boy," I hissed.

"Yeah, whatever. See you at school tomorrow and don't do anything I wouldn't do. Although, after yesterday, it looks like anything goes." With a wink, she marched off, leaving me with my mouth flapping like a pelican.

Recovering, I rushed over to Eli.

"So, what is it? How does the change affect her future?"

"We-e-ll."

"Oh, come on, don't drag it out!"

He grinned. "Everything's okay. Well, at the moment."

"Ugh?"

"Leah has changed but, I guess, she's not used to her new confidence because she makes a couple of mistakes with future boyfriends."

"She doesn't get pregnant, does she?"

"No, nothing like that. She just takes a chance on a couple of guys and her confidence is knocked a bit when it doesn't go right."

"Oh, poor Leah, just when she gets some courage, she loses it again. But she'll be okay, won't she?"

"Yes, she'll be fine. She goes to uni, just as she would have, but she gets better grades and ends up in a middle executive job, not too high flying but better than before. Her main influence is with her kids and grandkids. Their lives are different. One daughter becomes a judge who's really fair but gives tough sentences where needed. That changes things for a few other people."

"How?"

"I don't have every detail but one example is a woman who's alive who would've been killed if a violent man had received a shorter sentence, as he did in the original future. The woman doesn't have any more children afterwards, so there's no major change, except that she's around to support her family a lot longer than she would have been."

"Wow."

"One of Leah's grandsons becomes a popular teacher who inspires lots of kids to achieve more and another grandkid becomes a politician. All of this has caused some ripples in the future but because it's not that many generations away they're not major ones. They had to wait for the ripples to die down a bit before they could send Zac to me and me to you."

I smiled with relief. A rope that fastened around my heart three years ago had begun to fray. I didn't notice at the time, but now I realised it had begun to wear away after we saved Emma and now, having saved Leah, a strand had snapped. Maybe, if I helped enough people, the knot of guilt for failing my sister would finally unravel completely and I'd be free. I blinked back tears before they escaped. Life, without the ever-present guilt, would be amazing.

"Oh, and another thing." Eli grinned. "We're back on the mission to help Liam. Lisa lied about that as well, we were never taken off the case."

Something exploded inside me and I actually started bouncing.

"You mean, I haven't failed?"

"Nope." Eli was laughing now. "We can go tomorrow."

"Why not now?"

He shook his head. "There are still too many ripples originating in your time period, because of Leah. They had to up the power to get me here. They want us to be a bit further away from the 'inciting incident' before doing any more transporting. Tomorrow's early enough, anyway. Kian's not due to go missing for another three months."

"But Kian's in our time, so we don't need the Watchers."

"Kian's in *your* time, remember, not mine. The Watchers have to get me here and reset the time on the return journey so nobody misses us."

"Oh yeah, I keep forgetting."

"And there's something else; Lisa's been sacked."

"What?"

"She not a 'go-between' any more. The Watchers are real mad. She was taken on as an eight-year-old orphan from the past. They brought her forward to your generation and placed her with a training family, ex-Time Fixers. They've spent years training her up and now she's messed up and they can't use her any more."

"From the past? Wow! How far in the past?"

Eli smirked. "Well, let's say, it's when toilet flushing enemies was popular."

My shoulders sagged. "You know about that?"

The smirk grew. "I know everything, remember?"

"Not everything, you said."

He shrugged. "Most things then."

"You're a pain sometimes. You know that?"

"Part of my charm."

"So, go on, how do you know? There's no way my head-dunking threat is recorded in history."

"No, but I heard your friends talking before you joined them yesterday."

"Cheat!"

With his eyes sparkling, Eli seemed so friendly. At first, he'd been distant then angry with me, for shouting at Liam, but now he seemed more like a mate. Next step boyfriend? *I wish. I think.*

"Will Lisa get sent back now?"

Eli shook his head. "No, she was taken moments before her family's house burned down. Everybody back then thinks she's dead, which she would have been if they hadn't taken her out when they did. She has to stay here and live an ordinary life."

"That's not a bad thing." Still, I couldn't help feeling sorry for eight-year-old Lisa, losing her family that way.

"I'm just glad she's not our go-between any more. But I think you need to be careful; for eight years, half her life, she's been prepared for this job. Go-betweens are normally Fixers first but it sounds like they decided she wasn't cut out for that."

"I wonder why."

Eli smiled. "Anyway, just as she's started her new role, it's finished. It was an important job too, directing people, telling them what to do. From what you say, that's something she'd enjoy. And you're the reason it's ended."

"What?"

Eli held up his hands. "Not really, but that's how she'll see it, so be careful."

I grimaced. "I'm always careful around Lisa."

"Be extra careful."

Eli's words hung in the air as I walked home. Lisa's always hated me because I stand up to her but, now, losing her job and everyone cheering me for putting her down in the café …

I felt like cutting school, throwing a sicky and hiding out for a couple of weeks until she calmed down, if she ever would.

I stood no chance of that, though. First mention of feeling ill and Mum's out with the thermometer and Paracetamol. If there's no sign of a temperature, throwing up or limbs dropping off then to school I go.

***

And to school I went the next morning.

Feeling like a soldier on a recognisance mission, I walked through the school grounds scanning all sides. My friends stood in a tight group by the right-hand wall of the bottom yard. A last scan showed the area to be Lisa-free so I headed over to them.

Chad's arm was wrapped around Queenie's waist and Dwaine's tongue was down Tammy's throat.

By the time I reached them, Dwaine still hadn't come up for air. Queenie saw me looking and grinned.

"They're going for the world record."

"What? The world's longest kiss?"

"No, the deepest dive without oxygen."

"Ew!"

"I heard that," Tammy said, surfacing and licking her lips. Dwaine looked pretty satisfied as well.

"Next time, get a room," I said then instantly regretted it. I didn't want to encourage them. I'd already caused enough trouble with Leah.

"Better still, don't," Leah finished for me.

"Watch out," Queenie murmured, "Lisa alert."

Groups of chatting kids parted like the Red Sea as Lisa, BJ Becky, Lanky Melissa and Alana marched towards us.

"A word," Lisa said, her eyes pinpointing me like lazer probes.

"Goodbye? That's a word," I said.

"Now!"

I didn't want to go with her, and let people think she had power over me, but I guessed she'd be talking about Eli and the agency so I had no choice; I couldn't let anyone hear her.

"You've got one minute," I said and stepped away from the others.

"You think you're so clever, don't you?" she hissed, as soon as we were far enough away.

"No, I think I'm a normal human being, you're mixing me up with yourself."

"You've always got an answer. Smart-mouthed, Jess. Well, this time you've gone too far. Getting me kicked out of the agency was a big mistake."

"Er, actually, you did that."

Lisa ignored me. She didn't even pause for breath.

"I'm going to make you all pay and whatever happens, remember, it's your fault. Girls!"

With a final snarl she was gone, passing back through the crowds with her entourage like a celebrity, leaving me with icy fingers crawling down my spine. What did she mean, 'make us all pay'? What was she planning?

"So, what did she say?" Queenie hurried over and asked.

"Well, put it this way, I'm not on her Christmas card list and I'll have to watch my back, sides and every other direction."

"That's bad." Tammy shook her head.

"That's real bad," agreed Leah.

"You shouldn't have shown her up like that," Queenie moaned.

"Gee, thanks for your support."

"I'm only saying." Queenie shrugged.

"Yeah, well, don't bother. I'm not letting Lisa pick on me, Tammy or any of you, okay?"

"She threatened us all?" A worried frown darkened Tammy's forehead.

I nodded. "Sorry."

"I wish you'd let me move."

"We had to stand up to her, Tammy. We couldn't let her keep pushing us around."

"Why not?"

"Because it's not right. You've got to get a backbone!"

"You think I'm a coward?"

"No, it's hard to stand up to someone. Look, ignore me, we've got domestic science after registration, let's go beat up a couple of eggs."

Tammy smiled. "Only if I can crack 'em."

"It can be arranged."

***

I saw Lisa loads of times that day, she seemed to be everywhere. Each time, she smiled knowingly but did nothing. By the end of school I felt like my nerves were gonna snap. Whatever she was planning I just wished she'd get on with it.

***

"Hi Jess." Eli's voice stopped me as I walked through the open gates, chatting with my friends.

"Hi."

Why do I get a warm glow in my chest whenever I hear his voice?

"Let's leave the lovebirds in peace. See you tomorrow, Jess." Queenie said and walked away, tossing her tight plaits.

I scowled after her, knowing from the heat in my face that my cheeks were bright red again. I just hoped Eli hadn't heard her but with Queenie's voice the chances of that were like, nil.

Walking towards him, his grin told me he'd heard.

I decided not to comment because, knowing me, I'd only make things worse.

"Ready to go?" he asked.

"Yep," I answered, as bouncily as I could. "Have the time lines stopped moving?"

"You mean the time waves?"

"Yeah, them. Is everything okay?"

Eli nodded as he turned towards the bus stop. "Yeah, they've stopped and there's nothing too drastic. It's mostly Leah's own family who benefit."

Satisfied, I followed Eli onto a single-decker bus.

"So, what are we doing today?" I asked, as we took our seats.

"We're befriending Liam and hopefully getting him to connect with Kian."

"Are they in the same park?"

Eli nodded.

***

Forty minutes later, Eli slipped his arm around my waist as we stepped onto grass.

"Don't forget, boyfriend and girlfriend," he whispered.

"Hm, hmn." Was all I could manage. Electric sparks were shooting out from my waist and affecting my tongue; for some reason it had stuck to the roof of my mouth and wasn't going to move for anyone.

Eli pulled me closer, opened the tall, wired gate and led me across the pitch. Liam was kicking a football around with three other boys and Kian sat alone again, far from his brother. We walked over to our usual corner and sat with our backs against the fence.

It was a warm April day and thankfully the ground wasn't cold this time.

"Come on," Eli said, "We have to make this look good."

"Goal!" Liam shouted in the background.

Eli twisted so that his back was to the boys. He let his left arm rest on the floor on the other side of my legs and stroked my hair with his right hand. We were face to face, his lips close to mine and his minty, warm breath brushing my cheeks.

What if my breath smells foul? If he actually kisses me, this will be our first and I haven't even sucked a mint!

"Are you okay with this?" he whispered. I nodded and our lips met. It felt so good that every other thought evaporated. We were actually kissing, for real, and it was amazing. I mean, Eli's like, totally hot and kissing me! At that moment, it didn't matter whether it was for real or for the mission; all I knew was that I liked it, a lot. Finally, I understood Tammy and Dwaine; no wonder they never wanted to come up for air.

All too soon, it was over. Eli broke away and rested back against the railings, draping his arm around my shoulders and pulling me close.

"Was that okay?" he asked.

Okay, it was amazing! I'm glowing. If the sun goes down now, I'll light up the whole park.

"Yeah," I breathed.

"Good. I'm sorry I had to do that but it's for the mission, you know."

Eli's words flicked a switch and the lights blinked off. Instant power cut.

"Yeah, I know." My voice was as flat and dark as the inside of me. So, it was fake, he hadn't meant it at all. Maybe my breath did smell and it was a major sacrifice for him to play this part to save Liam. He was probably wishing I was Lisa, or some other girl, not plain, bad-breath me.

"I'm going to try and make contact now," Eli said, totally unaware of the devastation he'd caused. "Hey! Can I join your game?"

The boys stopped playing, looked at Eli then each other.

"That'd make our teams uneven." Liam squinted against the sun, just starting to drop in the early evening sky.

"That's all right, Jess'll play. Won't you, Jess?"

I could tell by the wiggly eyebrows and slight nod of his head that I was supposed to agree.

"Yeah," I said, "I'll play."

The boys all looked at one another with a 'here we go' expression. I felt the same, I mean, my complete knowledge of football was that two teams kick the ball into each other's goals. Oh yeah, and there's a goal keeper who just throws himself about. That's one position I *didn't* want.

"Right, okay." Liam grimaced like the decision caused him actual pain. "Well, this is Ashley, my brother." He pointed to a boy just slightly shorter than himself with the same dark hair and eyes. Both boys still wore their black school trousers and white shirts with damp patches under their arms.

"This is Kyle, you met him last time." Wearing a white T-shirt and baggy blue shorts, Kyle had obviously called at home before the park or he'd skipped school. He nodded. His head was shaved so close to his scalp that his brown hair was almost invisible.

"And this is Harry." Harry blinked blue eyes and hitched up his school trousers. With blond hair and big smile, he looked the friendliest of the lot.

"Hi," we both echoed.

"Right, Eli, you join my team and, Jess, you can join Ashley's."

"Hey, that's not fair!" Ashley argued. "You're only doing that so you'll win."

"No, I'm not."

"Yes, you are."

Way to make a girl feel welcome, guys.

"All right then, you have Eli and we'll have Jess."

I don't think Liam could've sounded less enthusiastic if he'd invited a plague-infested rat to join him. Still, it was for the mission and, after my tirade on our last encounter, I couldn't exactly have a strop about pre-judging women, especially as the next ten minutes proved me to be so inept at football a lame duck could have played better.

I got stuck in like everyone else, tackled Kyle, who happened to be on my team, and scored a home goal. I even cheered myself until I saw Liam's scowl and realised what I'd done. It didn't help that Eli creased over laughing and congratulated me for helping his team.

"That's my girl, help me win."

I scowled at him but he just kept on laughing.

After that, they didn't pass to me and if I did get possession of the ball it was tackled away from me immediately by the other team, or my own. Eli was especially good at stealing it from me. Some fake boyfriend he turned out to be!

Fifteen minutes was enough humiliation for me and at the next tackle I accidentally, on purpose, got knocked over and sat hugging my ankle.

"Are you all right?" Eli asked, rushing to my side. The attention was nice but not enough to get me back into that stupid game.

"I'll be okay," I said, trying to sound like a brave little soldier. "But I can't play."

"That's it then, sorry Eli." Liam shrugged.

"Kian could take my place," I suggested, brightly.

Liam's face darkened. "No way!"

Kian's head had lifted briefly but immediately dropped back onto his huddled knees.

"Why not?" Eli asked.

"'Cos he's, like, four-years-old," Liam's voice rang with sarcasm, "He's too young."

"He can't be any worse than me," I chirped.

"She's got a point," Eli agreed.

Gee thanks, flitted through my mind but I knew Eli had picked up on my plan and was going along with it.

"Come on, Liam. I want to play," Eli pushed.

"Oh, alright." Anybody would think we'd persuaded him to have electric shock treatment, he sounded so reluctant.

In an instant, Kian was on his feet, his face alight, running across the concrete towards us.

"I can play? Really?"

"Yeah, you'll have to be on my side. So much for a good game of footy," Liam grumbled.

Now, I'd love to report that Kian played like a pro and Liam was totally impressed but, let's face it, that was never gonna happen. Kian sucked, big time, but he was no worse than me and he didn't score any home goals. In fact, he even managed to get one in the right net which, yeah, technically made him better than me.

"Hey, way to go, kid!" Eli enthused, giving Kian a high five.

I knew what Eli was doing and joined in, cheering him on.

"Well done, Kian, thanks for taking my place," I said, at the end.

"Is your leg better?" he asked, big innocent eyes making me want to hug him.

"Yeah, loads better, thanks."

I actually remembered to limp as we walked away.

"So, did we do okay?" I asked, as soon as we were out of earshot.

"I reckon we did good," Eli said with a grin. "We've a long way to go but by the middle of the game

Liam stopped grumbling at the kid and even passed the ball to him a couple of times. It's a good start."

"Great," I said, loving the warm glow in my chest.

Maybe, just maybe, we could actually save them.

***

CHAPTER SIXTEEN - GONE

"So, when do we go again?" I asked, as soon as we stepped off the bus.

"I don't know, Zac will tell me. This mission is a bit different because we're working in 'real time'."

"Ugh?"

Eli sighed, like he was explaining it to a dunce. "You're not travelling in time to see them, they're on the same date and time as you. If we turn up too often, when we don't live in Mexborough, Liam will get suspicious; so, we might have to wait a few days before we go back. On the other hand, the Watchers might send us forward in time so we can go straight away."

"Oh," I said, understanding about half of it. This time travel stuff seemed to skim the surface of my brain like skaters on ice. "Okay, so I'll wait until you turn up then?"

A huge part of me wanted Eli to say he'd turn up anyway just to see me but dream on, Jess.

"Yeah," he said, "I'll be in touch when we can go."

"Okay."

As I watched him walk away, I remembered our kiss. If only it had been real, if only he'd wanted to kiss me again and not because of the mission.

Oh, shut up, Jess. Since when did you go all gooey over a boy?

But I knew the answer to that; it was the first day I laid eyes on Eli. Even while he stood watching me being beaten up, I fancied him, no matter how much I fought my hormones betrayed me and there wasn't a thing I could do about it.

***

The next day was Thursday which meant double Maths in the morning and a History test after first break, so it wasn't exactly my best day of the week, and Lisa made it worse. She was still giving me knowing grins, full of confidence. I mean, I could cope with her being nasty, that's normal, but her smiling and saying 'Hello, Jess,' made me feel like a fawn being eyed up by a lioness. She was probably trying to psych me out and it was working, big time.

Doing a history test with my mind consumed with Kian, Eli and Lisa was not a recipe for success. I stared at the questions, my eyes reading them but my brain totally uncomprehending. They could've been written in Swahili for all I understood.

I came out of there convinced I'd flunked and I still had to get through Phys. Ed. and French before the torture ended.

When I'd finally served my sentence, I didn't bother waiting for my friends but headed straight for the gates. Looking first up then down the road, my hope dropped like a pound in a vending machine.

"Hey, not waiting for us? Too eager to see your boyfriend?" Tammy taunted.

I turned and grinned at them.

"I've told you, he's not my boyfriend but he is more interesting to look at then you lot."

"I think he heard that," Leah said, smiling.

"Yeah, pull the other one."

"No, really." Leah pointed behind me.

I turned and there was Eli, leaning against the railings, as usual, wearing a very wide grin. My stomach twisted and fluttered at the same time; not an easy task. Why didn't I have the ability to know when to keep my mouth shut?

"Go to your lover-boy," Queenie teased, her arm clamped around Chad.

I turned back and thumped her arm.

"Okay, Torment, I'm going."

Queenie smirked then walked away with the others.

Taking a deep breath to calm my jittery stomach, I turned then stopped. Eli had gone.

My heart thumped then quit. What was going on? Had I embarrassed him by saying he was interesting to look at? But he hadn't looked bothered, in fact, he'd looked amused.

"Jess." Eli's disembodied voice reached me first then he appeared right in front of me.

"Aargh! What're you doing? You nearly gave me a heart attack!" I said, clutching my chest. "What if someone saw you do that?"

I glanced around, quickly. Thankfully, no one seemed to be looking in our direction, even though they were still streaming out of the gates like water from a hose.

"Jess, there's trouble." Eli's voice was urgent. "Something's just happened. Time's shifting, fast, now. Don't know if they can keep me …"

He'd gone again, vanished like a hallucination.

"Eli?"

What did he mean, there's trouble? What trouble? Where? He said time was shifting but why? And it's dangerous to travel when there are waves. Was he in danger? Could he get lost in time?

What if I never see him again? The thought exploded in my head and sent chills through my entire body.

I stood, waiting, my head spinning from side to side, watching for him.

Come back, Eli. Please come back! I urged, silently.

"Jess."

Eli's voice sounded far away, his image slowly solidifying before me. I didn't even stop to think what people would make if it. My focus was solely on him.

"Zac's managed to reach me. It's bad. You've got to go to Mexborough," he said, his body still strangely transparent in places.

"Why? What do you want me to do?"

"Kian's gone; three months early. Something's caused a change. Find …"

He'd gone again. What could have happened? Kian had disappeared early, but why? How? And why would three months make so much difference in the future?

"… get him back." Eli's disjointed voice was there but no body.

"But how?"

"Don't know… wing it… important. Good lu…"

He'd gone. I waited but there was nothing else. I had to get to Mexborough but didn't even know the times of the buses and had no idea what to do when I got there.

Setting off towards Blythe Avenue I fished out my mobile and rang Mum.

"Mum, is it okay for me to go to Leah's for tea?"

"Yes, that's fine. What time will you be back?"

No idea.
"Er, about seven?"
"Okay, have you got any homework?"
"Only Maths. I can do that when I get in."
"Make sure you do. Okay, see you later."
I ended the call then speed-dialled Leah.
"Hi, Leah, can you cover for me? I'm at yours for tea."
"Ooh, are things getting interesting with Eli?"
"You could say that."
"Okay, I'll cover but I want details tomorrow."
Yeah, well that really could be interesting.
I reached the bus stop and stood waiting. I was pretty impressed with myself for figuring out that the Watchers wouldn't be able to re-adjust time on my journey back and had actually organised an alibi. I just hoped the Watchers were able to keep Eli safe. Seeing him disappear then re-appear partially transparent had really freaked me out.
I stuck out my hand for the first bus to arrive.
"Do you go to Highwoods Road in Mexborough?" I asked, as the door clanked open. The driver shook his head.
I don't even know what bus I'm supposed to catch or how often they run. How am I supposed to even get to Mexborough? Anything could be happening and I'm stuck here at the bus stop!
Right then and there, I decided that in future I would pay more attention. Eli had always led us to the right bus, at the right time, and I'd just let him. Now, without him, I couldn't even reach Kian. Sobs lodged in my throat and I swallowed them down.
You can't lose it now, Jess. You've got to hold it together.

Another bus crested the hill and I stuck out my arm.

"Do you go to Highwoods Road, Mexborough?"

This time the driver nodded and I nearly cried with relief. I stepped on board, flashed my travel pass and gratefully sank into the nearest seat. I spent the next forty minutes trying to figure out what to do, but as Mexborough approached, I still had no idea.

***

With no other choice, I got off at the usual stop and rushed to the park.

One glance told me that Liam and his friends weren't there. The park was empty.

"Jess."

My heart leapt so high it nearly blocked my throat. Spinning around, I found Eli standing behind me, just inside the park.

"Eli! How did you get here? Are you staying?"

He shook his head and spoke quickly.

"The Watchers told me to catch a bus here, then where to stand. They boosted the power to transport me in time but we only have seconds. Some information is coming through. Liam collected Kian from school. He walked with his friends while Kian trailed behind; the next time Liam looked Kian was gone. CCTV shows him with a teenaged girl and boy but their faces aren't clear. In twenty minutes. there's a struggle. Kian runs into the dual carriageway near the train station. A car swerves across the middle divide to avoid him and crashes into the side of a bus coming the other way. Seven people are killed including Kian, who is hit by the next car. In the confusion the teens slip away. We don't know much more because time lines are still changing but one of those killed is a young man who will be the grandfather of the guy who invents time travel. Once that wave hits there'll be no more ...."

He was gone. I stared at the spot where he'd stood.

What had he said? He'd gabbled everything so quickly it was hard to take it all in. Kian has been taken by teenagers, a girl and boy. For some reason, he runs away from them, into the road, and causes an accident that wouldn't normally happen. So, seven people die who should live and that's what caused the time waves. But what was the last thing he said? One of the victims is the grandfather of the person who invents time travel and when that wave hits there'll be no more ... what? My brain connected with a jolt. There'll be no time travel, no Time Agency, no Watchers, no Time Fixers, no one else will be helped and I'll never see Eli again.

I felt as though I'd been hit by a bull dozer. This couldn't all end here and what about the things time travel has already done?

What about Emma? Will she die now because our trips to her won't have happened? But I still remember her. I remember every conversation. Will I forget everything from the last few weeks? Will I forget Eli? I shook my head. This was way too much for my small brain to take in. Even a genius would struggle.

Eli said that wave hadn't reached them yet. Did he mean it hadn't reached the Watchers or his own time, whenever he came from?

Stop! Focus. What do I know? It happens on the dual carriageway. I've got to get there before Kian and the mystery teens. I have to stop him running out into the road. But how can I do that? I've no idea where to even find the dual carriageway.

***

CHAPTER SEVENTEEN – AGAINST TIME

If only I'd known where the accident happened!
My bus had travelled along the dual carriageway today. I even remember seeing a sign for the station, near a pedestrian crossing, but after that the bus meandered around a housing estate before arriving on Highwoods Road. There was no way I could retrace its route. If I'd known, I could have stepped off at the bus station, at the bottom of the carriageway, then I would have been there, ready to save Kian.

Eli didn't appear again and twenty minutes didn't give me time to hang around. Looking across the park, I could see a pub and a busy road. Hopefully, the road was busy enough to lead to the dual carriageway without me trying to find my way through a housing estate.

I ran across the grass, through a thin line of trees and out onto the pavement.

Two forty-ish men, each holding a pint of beer, stood in the entrance to the pub.

I cupped my hands to my mouth and yelled.
"Excuse me!"
They were busy talking and didn't reply.
"Excuse me!" I yelled louder.
The shorter of the two, a bald man with very baggy jeans, turned towards me.

"Which way is the railway station?"
"That way!" He pointed to my left.
"Thanks!"

I'd no idea how far I had to go but there were only seventeen minutes left to get there.

After sprinting past a row of bungalows, I stood at a crossroads, hopping from foot to foot.

"Come on!" I urged the steady stream of cars. "Let me cross!"

Finally, the traffic gave me a break and I raced on down a hill, past terraced houses.

I dodged a group of kids then found the pavement blocked by a mobility scooter. Glancing over my shoulder, I figured there was just about time to step into the road, and back, before an advancing white van clipped me. Wrong. The blasting horn vibrated inside me and I felt a swirl of air as the van swerved to avoid me. I jumped back onto the pavement, my legs wobbly.

That was way too close. Watch out, Jess, or you won't be alive to help Kian.

I took a moment to let my pulse slow down and catch my breath, before setting off again past more houses, a shop and a Chinese takeaway.

When I reached another crossroads, I paused. Traffic was too heavy again. The junction had lights so I pressed the button, urging the standing red man to turn into the walking green one.

Ahead the road forked, one going left between shops and the other going right between the back of the shops and a row of houses.

Which way?

The road to the right looked wider and busier but was it the right one?

I glanced at my watch; six minutes gone, only fourteen to go.

This is crazy. I'm never gonna make it.

I spotted a girl about my age, across the road, her thumbs flying across her smartphone. As soon as the little green man appeared, I raced over and yelled.

"Which way to the station?"

"That way," she said, pointing to the right.

"Thanks!"

Keep going, Jess, just keep going.

My breath came in short gasps as I passed a couple of buildings before glancing over my shoulder. The road was clear so I dodged across to a triangle of grass, dividing the two routes.

There was no pavement, at first, just a narrow line of worn-down grass but I didn't care so long as it took me where I wanted to go.

With every stride I was aware of the seconds passing and when the road curved to the left, revealing a large roundabout with the dual carriageway on the other side, my eyes stung with relief.

I blinked back tears and, with my heart hammering like a demented lumberjack, I kept going. Stitch pierced my side, I felt sure there wasn't enough oxygen in the world to fill my lungs and take away the pain in my legs but still I pushed on. The roads around this roundabout were really busy and a precious minute, that felt more like ten, passed without me getting anywhere.

"Come on," I urged, as one car after another sped around and up the road I needed to cross. "Come on!"

Finally, there was a gap and I took it. Racing on, I reached a slip road curving away to my left. It led to several long bus stops; the place I could have left my bus, if only I'd known.

As I ran across the slip road, I saw a little boy crying, his blond curls bouncing, as a round woman, in too-tight jeans and flowing top, dragged him away from the stops.

"Shut up! You're doing my head in!" she yelled, giving his arm a sharp tug.

My fists clenched.

"Kian!" I called, running towards them. "Kian!"

The woman just kept on walking, her deep voice ranting.

"Keep hold of my hand. Do you hear me? You let go again and I'm gonna tan your backside."

My nails dug into my palms. How could she be so evil, kidnapping a little kid then shouting at him for being upset and trying to get away from her?

"Let him go!" I yelled, as I finally drew level with them and grabbed the woman's arm.

She spun towards me, her face fierce, and as she did the little boy turned too. It wasn't Kian.

"Just who do you think you are?" the woman shouted. "You keep your hands off me!"

"I'm sorry," I said, holding up my hands in submission. "I thought you were someone else. I'm really sorry."

My cheeks felt like I had a major sunburn as I backed away.

"So you should be!" my victim shouted, "You'd better watch out if you ever touch me again!"

Blimey, at this rate I might as well put a target on my back and give all the people who hate me somewhere to aim. I'm such an idiot, Eli said the kidnappers were a teenage girl and boy but from behind that kid looked so like Kian. You've got to do better, Jess. Come on, focus.

I set off running again, glancing at my watch; there were less then five minutes left and no sign of Kian.

Where is he?

Tears blurred my vision.

I'm not going to make it. He's not here.

I tried to remember what Eli had told me. He said it happened near the train station.

But where's the station? I made my mind replay my bus journey. *It was after the stops and near a crossing. Where's the crossing?*

Suddenly aware of traffic, I wondered with every passing car whether it was the one.

Thankfully, I finally saw the crossing, about 100 metres in front of me. A wall on my left had a raised, narrow road running behind it with the backs of buildings on the other side. A young couple with a little boy emerged from a gap between the buildings. They were about thirty metres ahead and their backs were towards me as they crossed the narrow road and walked quickly on until the wall was a little lower. The older boy, wearing an anorak with the hood up, jumped down onto the pavement then lowered the little boy down beside him.

The little boy's monkey mask slid up as he was lowered, knocking back his hood and revealing a mass of blond curls.

I froze and, even though my lungs were bursting, I felt like I'd stopped breathing.

Coming to my senses, I shouted. "Kian!"

Kian turned, a grin appearing below the mask as I ran towards him.

"Jess!" he cried, "Look at my new car!"

He held out a shiny, red, toy car and started towards me but the older boy grabbed his arm, looked my way and smirked.

"Jake!"

"Yeah, Jake." The girl jumped down in front of them and blocked my path. "Get out of here, Jess!"

"Lisa?" Wearing tatty jeans and a blue hoodie that covered her hair, I hadn't recognised her.

The world seemed to pause while I tried to process the information. Lisa and Jake were the kidnappers but why?

Me.

The realisation hit me like a bolt of electricity. Lisa was doing this to wreck my mission and get back at me for the café incident. Jake had joined her because I'd come between him and Leah. Kian and all those people could die because of me. But how did they do it? Kian was taken straight after school and I came on the first bus. Of course, they must have skipped the last period. That would be on record when they looked for the kidnappers though, didn't they care if they were caught?

"Lisa, you have to let Kian go," I said, desperately.

"I don't have to do anything," Lisa said. "Haven't you heard? I got the sack. Now I can do exactly as I like."

"But I've seen you both. If you go ahead with this, your lives will be ruined."

"My life was ruined years ago." Lisa's voice sounded cold and empty.

I glanced at Jake, not sure how much to say in front of him or how much Lisa had already told him. But then, if I failed there'd be no time travel anyway so talking about it couldn't do any harm.

"Lisa, you don't understand. If you don't stop now there'll be an accident, people will die, time travel won't happen."

Lisa sneered. "Who told you that? Your little boyfriend, Eli? Where is he, anyway?"

"He can't come; time travel has already been affected."

"Boo woo. Time waves, you've got to love them." Lisa grinned. "It's working already."

"What?"

She knew that her actions would affect the future? But, of course she did, she'd been trained for years.

"I bet they're panicking now, the almighty Watchers. They think they can do whatever they want with people's lives and never pay for it. Well, this is going to shake them up. Did you know their government doesn't know about them? Well, they will. When I've dealt with the kid, I'm going to write a letter, send it to the post office and ask them to deliver it on the right date in the future. You've seen that done in films and, just in case that doesn't work, when I'm old I'm going to tell all. When the government finds out, they'll shut them down and take their technology because of the mess they're making. A girl they snatched from the past, who used to be such a good little girl, has now become the kidnapper of a little boy who will just disappear. They'll never know that he was going to go missing anyway because history will already be changed. Who knows how many other messes I can create in my lifetime too, none of them meant to happen in original history." Her eyes sparkled with excitement. "I'm going to ruin the Watchers"

Everything except Lisa, Kian and Jake faded into the background. I no longer heard the sound of traffic or even noticed the road. I had to find a way to stop her, that was my only focus now.

"But, if you go ahead, one of the people killed is the ancestor of the inventor of time travel. No one else will be helped."

Lisa, whooped, "Excellent! This is easier than I thought, I won't even have to write any letters. I'll destroy them and their Agency. I'll stop you seeing your precious Eli, as well. Time travel won't even be invented? Wow! Better than I thought!"

I bit my lip, quickly pushing Eli's image aside. Kian mattered now and Liam and Ashley and anyone else who ever needed help. I had to figure out a way to persuade her.

"You'll still be in the past," I blurted.

"What?"

"If there's no time travel everything will unravel. You'll end up back in the past, where you began, and die in that fire." I had no idea whether that would really happen but it sounded right and I had to try something.

Jake had been holding a wriggling Kian and watching us both, like a tennis match, but now he spoke up.

"What're you both going on about? Come on, Lisa, forget this rubbish and let's go. If we hang about here, we'll get caught; you promised we wouldn't get caught."

"Just a minute, Jake," Lisa ordered. "You think you know everything, Jess. We only have the Watchers' word that my family died. How do I know it's true? I know there was a fire but, when everything vanished in front of me, they were still alive. They might have survived, but if they didn't I'd rather have died with them, anyway. The Watchers brought me to this time and put me with a new 'family'. Why couldn't they have brought my own family, if they could bring me? They took everything from me. I didn't know anything about this century. The new 'family' home schooled me until I was eleven. They taught me about current times and the Agency. They actually thought they were doing me a favour."

"They were, they saved you."

"Are you both nuts?" Jake said, scowling. "Come on, we're gonna get nicked!"

"Shut up, Jake! By the time I went to school I had no idea how to get along with other kids. They all had their friends; I'd been with adults for years and, before that, with children from a completely different era. I was bullied, laughed at when I got things wrong, things the new 'family' forgot to tell me about the present day or about things any 'normal' kid would know." Each time Lisa said the word 'family' she spat it out like poison. "I hated them but decided I wouldn't let them get away with it. I'd beat them. I played along, being the happy little rescued kid. I learned how to fit in at school, picking on others instead of being picked on. Being beautiful and sexy so everyone followed me. You're all like sheep in this century, so easy to lead and fool."

I frowned but was happy to keep her talking; with any luck, I could delay everything long enough to allow the bus, carrying the ancestor of time travel, to pass. Then I'd just have to figure out a way to save Kian.

"What are you planning to do to Kian? He's only a little kid, he hasn't hurt anyone, why don't you let him go?"

"Oh, no, I have plans for him. I'm pretty good with computers, not that I let anyone know it. I've used my friends' computers to search some pretty extreme sites on the dark web. Oh, and I've deleted the history. I bought an unregistered phone; a burner phone they call it on TV. There are people out there who will pay a fortune for a cute little boy like him. It's all arranged."

"You're evil." I couldn't find any other words.

Lisa just gave a smile that made my insides twist.

"Don't do it, Jake. Don't have any part of this. You can stop her!" Back when Jake was threatening Leah, I would never have dreamed that, just a few days later, I'd be begging him for help, but I had to try everything.

"Why would I stop her? There's money in this for both of us and I get to see you look so pathetic. What's it feel like to lose?"

"We're going on a train now, aren't we, Kian?" Lisa crooned.

"No!" he shouted and kicked Jake's ankle.

"Ow!" Jake yelled. "You little ...!" Taken by surprise he lost his grip on Kian, who set off running towards me.

"Oh no, you don't," Lisa yelled.

Still between Kian and me she opened her arms to catch him.

Kian veered left to escape her. His foot hit the edge of the pavement.

A car horn sounded.

***

CHAPTER EIGHTEEN - COLISION

"Kian, no!"

I was helpless as Kian stumbled off the pavement and into the road, causing a silver BMW to swerve around him.

My body felt like ice, expecting to hear the sickening thud of metal on flesh at any second; or the crash of a car hitting an oncoming bus.

"Come here you mongrel!" Lisa yelled, running towards him.

He rose onto his toes ready to dash away from her, further into the road.

"No, Kian, come to me!" I shouted, holding out my arms. Kian took his eyes off Lisa and ran towards me as a red Vauxhall sped past, its horn blaring. Lisa made a dive for him but he dodged and only her fingertips touched his coat before I snatched him up into my arms.

"You witch!" Lisa yelled, stumbling back onto the pavement to a last angry car horn. She gave them the finger then headed for me, followed closely by Jake.

Putting Kian down, I pushed him behind me.

"Give him to me!" Lisa ordered.

"It's all over, Lisa," I said, "You lost. Even if you take him now there are loads of witnesses, you'll never get away with it."

"What witnesses? What did they see, a girl in a hoodie and a boy in an anorak? Neither of us look anything like this normally."

"I'll tell," I said.

"Not if you're not able," she said with a grin.

Suddenly Jake lunged for me. He grabbed my right arm, wrenching hard, while Lisa went for Kian.

"Run, Kian!" I shouted. "And don't go on the road!

From the edge of my vision, I saw him hesitate then set off back down the pavement, towards the bus stops, his little legs flying.

Lisa chased after him while Jake's free arm wrapped around my waist.

"Got you now!" he said as I wriggled and twisted, trying to break free. "You're gonna pay for all your interfering."

"Let me go!" I shouted, bucking like a wild horse. I had to get free; I'd saved Kian once but there was still a chance he could run back into the road.

My panicked brain cells remembered something from a film. S.I.N.G. Jamming my left elbow backwards into his **S**olar plexus, I heard Jake gasp. Immediately, I kicked my heel onto the **I**nstep of his foot. I wasn't really sure what the instep was but it involved slamming my foot down on his and that was good enough for me. Then I rammed the same foot backwards onto his k**N**eecap.

"Aargh!" he cried, as much in anger as pain, but he'd released me so I spun around and kneed him in the **G**roin.

He crumpled. I didn't have time to enjoy my victory; Lisa had almost reached Kian. I sped after them, leaving Jake in a heap on the floor.

About thirty metres from the bus stops, Lisa caught up with Kian and wrestled him into her arms. A bus was loading passengers but a wall stopped them seeing the little boy in trouble, just metres away. Passing drivers would only see a young boy running off and his older sister chasing and catching him; normal childlike behaviour, nothing to worry about.

Kian struggled, just as I had with Jake, but stood no chance of breaking free.

I sped up, my lungs burning.

"Let … him … go," I panted when I'd nearly reached them.

"Or what?" she snarled. "Stop there or I'll hurt him…"

I stopped two metres away, holding out my arms in a gesture of peace.

"Good idea of mine, hey?" she went on. "Wreck your mission by making the kid disappear, way before it was meant to happen, put all those Watchers out of a job and stop you seeing Eli. Triple payback! And, from what you say, destroy time travel in the process. Bonus!"

"But what about Kian? He's only a kid. He's never hurt you."

"So? Who cares? I hate kids and he was going to disappear, anyway."

She's crazy! How can I stop her?

"Lisa, just let him go, please." I tried my gentlest, most persuasive voice, while edging slowly forwards. "You can find another way to get back at us. I'll do anything you want, just let him go."

Lisa grinned. "Anything?"

"Yes," I said, my stomach fluttering at the thought of what she might demand. "Anything."

Lisa's grin vanished. "Then save him!"

In one move, she lifted Kian off his feet and flung him to her right, out into the road. I'd been so focussed on her, I hadn't noticed the bus leave the stop but obviously Lisa had. It had pulled out and picked up speed. Now it was only metres from Kian.

I didn't have time to think; I just reacted and ran out into the road. To the squeal of brakes, I scooped Kian up, spun around and threw him back towards the pavement. The move left me off-balance and I couldn't do anything as the front of the yellow bus closed in on me.

Time seemed to slow down as my mind processed every millisecond: my arms coming up to my head, the shocked look on the grey-haired driver's face, the detail on the huge grill bearing down on me, two hands thumping me hard from behind, pain shooting through my back as I found myself propelled towards the pavement, pain in my hands and knees as I landed, rolled and heard a thud behind me.

My roll turned me just in time to see Eli flung into the air by the impact and landing several metres away.

My heart jolted.

"Eli!" I heard myself scream.

For an instant, he lay there terrifyingly still and twisted with blood on his face, then he was gone. He just vanished.

Voices sounded around me.

"It was her; she threw him."

"This girl saved him."

"Where's the boy? I hit someone; where is he? I know I hit someone. He saved the girl."

"There is no boy. Maybe, it was the girl you hit."

"Are you alright, Love? Did the bus hit you?"

The voices went on; I'd no idea how many people were around me. My eyes only focussed on a patch of road, four metres away, where a smear of blood slowly dried in the early evening sun.
***

CHAPTER NINETEEN - ELI

Nothing reached me. Their voices were just background static as my head replayed those final few seconds; the sickening thud, Eli tossed in the air like a matador's cape, him lying on the ground, battered and bleeding.

Lights shone in my eyes.

"She's in shock; let's get her into the ambulance."

Hands helped me to my feet and led me behind the bus to a waiting ambulance. My eyes stayed focussed on the point where Eli had lain until the bus obscured my view. Still I looked, as though hoping to penetrate the yellow metal.

I was vaguely aware as they helped me into the ambulance and sat me down. Something was strapped to my arm, it tightened and released before being removed. Through the open doors, I saw Lisa and Jake being led away by two police officers.

Kian, where's Kian?

A moment of panic filtered through my addled brain before I saw him being led past by a female police officer, his little hand in hers. Before I could call to him, the doors of the ambulance slammed shut.

***

Later, I sat in a hospital side room with dressings on my knees and hands, cradling a cup of sweet tea, while Eli's prostrate form still filled my mind.

"Oh, Jess, are you all right, Love?" Mum's voice reached me before the door had fully opened; within seconds I was wrapped in her arms, my cup tipping dangerously. I set it down on a low table in front of me. "What happened, Sweety? Look at your poor hands and knees. Are they badly grazed? How did it happen? You were supposed to be at Leah's. What were you doing in Mexborough? And where's Leah? Jessica? Jessica."

Her insistent questioning finally drew me out of my daze. A small room with blue walls and two brown faux-leather settees came into focus.

"I'm alright, Mum," I managed.

"But what happened, Jess?" Mum had taken the seat next to me and leaned forwards to peer into my face. With wide eyes, uncombed hair and a frown creasing her forehead, she looked nothing like the tough, no-nonsense Mum I knew. "Why were you in Mexborough and who was that girl who tried to hurt that little boy?"

"She's a girl from school," I murmured.

"Leah?"

"No!"

"A friend?"

"No!" That's one thing Lisa would never be. Even the thought made me cringe.

"They say she pushed him in front of a bus. Is that true? Why would she do that?"

I shrugged. How could I explain everything to Mum?

"They say you saved him."

The picture of Eli came back, along with a sick feeling in my stomach.

"You were so brave, Darling. I'm proud of you. But you could have been killed."

Killed. The words stung my brain. *Is Eli dead? He'd looked it, lying there so still.* Emptiness filled my heart. *He saved me. Is he in hospital somewhere? Are doctors working on him or is he ... gone? What if I never see him again? What if I never find out what happened to him?*

The police came in, interrupting my morbid thoughts and asking loads of questions. I explained that I had met Kian and Liam by chance and got to know them; that way, my story would match any answers the boys gave. I just hoped Kian and Liam didn't mention Eli. I couldn't give the police Eli's full name because I didn't know it and, even if I did, they couldn't turn up at the present-day Eli's house: I had no idea how young the current day Eli was and he definitely wouldn't know anything about me.

I made up a story about overhearing Lisa and Jake plotting to kidnap Kian and that I'd gone to make sure he was okay. When they asked how I'd managed to avoid the bus hitting me, I told them I'd jumped clear. It made me feel like a traitor; Eli was the hero, not me, but how could I explain about Eli and how he'd disappeared? The police seemed satisfied, thankfully, and after a few more questions we were able to leave. Mum led the way to our car and we drove home in silence.

I spent the evening in my room, staring at the opposite wall but seeing only Eli. Nothing mattered to me now, not my laptop, on its workstation by the door, nor my Wii and TV, over by the window. Only Eli mattered now. I had to know whether he was alive.

***

"You should stay home today, Honey," Mum said, the next morning. "It's the last day before the Easter Holidays, anyway. It won't hurt to miss a day after all you've been through. You'll be fine by the time the holidays are over."

Blimey, I must look bad if Mum wants me to miss school!

My uniform lay beside me on the bed but I hadn't been able to put it on. I was desperate to know about Eli but if I arrived at school and he wasn't there or, worse, if Zac was there instead with bad news, I don't know what I'd do. I knew that, in normal time, Eli would be hurt too badly to be out and about the very next day but, as he was from the future, he could wait until he was well and then travel back to see me today, couldn't he? So, if he wasn't there… Tears welled in my eyes, as Mum watched me with the same concerned frown she'd worn the day before. She was tidy now, her wavy, brown hair combed, her minimal makeup in place and her beige trousers and blouse unruffled. She came and joined me on the bed, moving my uniform out of the way.

"I know you're not up to school after all that happened yesterday, it was such a shock, but you could do with some fresh air. I have to do some shopping. Why don't you join me?"

I blinked back the tears and shook my head.

"I might go out later."

"Alright, Love." Mum stroked my hair and gave me a sympathetic smile. "If you need to talk, I'm here. Okay?"

I nodded.

"I'll be off then; I won't be long."

Five minutes later she called up to say she was leaving. I heard the front door click and her car start up.

I drew up my knees and sat chewing my nails. Not knowing was killing me. If Eli was okay, I wanted to find out but if he wasn't … My thoughts were like a tennis ball batted backwards and forwards across my mind, do I go or not?

Mum had returned from the shops before I finally plucked up enough courage to climb off my bed, comb my hair and put on some makeup.

"You can do this," I told my reflection.

"I'm going out, Mum, just for a bit."

"Alright, Love. Don't be too long though; you don't want to overdo it."

"I won't. See you later."

My stomach spun like a Ferris wheel as I turned onto Haugh Road then stopped dead. Eli wasn't there. The road outside school was quiet; it was eleven a.m. and everyone was in class.

You're an idiot, Jess. Why didn't you come this morning? How's Eli supposed to know to come now? School will have marked me absent for today so he may not come at all or would the Watchers figure out I'd be here when no one's around?

Cold panic whipped through my body. This was the last day before the Easter holidays; if I didn't see Eli today, I would have to wait two weeks before school opened again. Swallowing down the lump in my throat, I walked to Eli's usual spot, my heart tightening with every step. I touched the railings where he always leaned, blinking as pressure built behind my eyes.

"Please come, Eli." I lost the battle and tears leaked onto my cheeks, "Please be okay."

"Hello, Jess."

Spinning towards the voice, my wide smile instantly dropped.

Zac stood in the gap leading to the fields where Lisa had beaten me up, nearly five weeks ago.

"I've been waiting for you."

His green shirt, only half buttoned, revealed chest hairs, dyed purple, and his hands rested in the pockets of his green and purple striped trousers. I blinked; he looked like an escapee from the circus.

But it wasn't his clothes that bothered me as I crossed the road to meet him.

"Where's Eli?"

Zac's violet eyes examined me.

"You really care for him, don't you?"

I wiped away the tears and nodded.

"He's okay or, at least, he will be. Well actually, in my time, he's fine."

"What?"

"As a result of the accident, Eli had concussion, two fractured ribs, a broken arm and a badly bruised leg."

I gasped. "You said he was okay!"

"In my time he is and in your time he hasn't had the accident yet."

I closed my eyes.

"Zac, you're not making sense."

"I'm making perfect sense but you don't understand me. The Eli you know comes from a couple of years in your future."

"A couple of years?"

Finally, an answer to one of my questions.

"Yes, and that Eli will be out of action for a few weeks. He won't be able to come back and see you until after his recovery."

"But once he's well, he could come back to right now. He could appear at the side of me, all well again."

"He could, but I need to speak to you and it would be better for you not to see this Eli for a little while."

"Why?"

"Because …"

"Are you punishing us? We haven't done anything wrong, have we?" I could feel my insides heating up ready to burst and hit someone, namely, Zac if he didn't let me see Eli.

"No, not at all."

"Then why? Your agency does time travel, they could send me into the future to visit him, instead."

Zac shook his head. "Not possible."

"Why not?"

Zac's smile was sad, "Because you are not allowed to see the future; plus, his family and friends are with him, explaining your presence would be awkward."

"I'll make something up, anything!" I felt like grabbing his green lapels and threatening to throttle him unless he took me to Eli. "Why won't you let me see him?"

I took several deep breaths, trying to calm my emotions.

"You will, soon, let me explain…"

"When? And anyway, why did the Watchers let him get hurt? They must have known what would happen if they sent him back. Why didn't they let the bus hit me? It would only have been the same result. I would have been hurt instead of Eli."

"No, Jess, it wouldn't have been the same. Eli is stronger than you. Time lines were fluctuating but the Watchers caught a glimpse of the outcome, you were killed when the bus hit you."

"Killed?"

"Yes. You saved time travel when you drew Kian to you near the station and prevented a major traffic accident; but time altered again when you rescued him from the bus and put yourself in its path. You were never meant to die at that time; you wouldn't even have been there if it wasn't for us and the changes Lisa made. Your death caused waves to erupt again, changes in your family, the lives you will help while you work for us. All of this altered the future. Eli was given the chance to save you and everyone your life will touch. The Watchers told him that it would be difficult getting him to the exact place and time because of the waves. They also explained that they didn't know whether he would survive the accident but he did stand a better chance than you because he's older and stronger. In his own time, he travelled to the spot and stepped out at exactly the right moment for the Watchers to transport him. Thankfully, the road in Eli's time was not so busy."

"He chose to be hurt instead of me?" I swallowed a rock in my throat.

Zac smiled, "He had his reasons."

"What reasons?" My voice was barely more than a whisper.

"He'll need to tell you those himself."

Does he love me? I felt my face flush at the thought.

"What about when he was transported to his own time after the accident? He was lying in the road; he could have been run over again."

Zac shook his head. "The Watchers transported him to that location in the late evening, when the road was quiet, and a couple of our past Fixers, who work in the ambulance service, were there to pick him up."

"But, how were his injuries explained in his time? What did they say happened to him?"

"A hit and run driver – who will never be found, of course, as he doesn't exist."

"But how did they arrange it so quickly?"

"Normally, they would have lots of time because they are in the future but, on this occasion, they had to act quickly because if you died then we'd also lose Eli. So, they sent me back to speak to Eli and the ambulance guys as a matter of urgency. It was quite risky, travelling while all those waves were still so erratic. I kept fading in and out, that was one weird feeling, but I managed to tell them everything they needed to know with just seconds to spare."

"What do you mean, if I died, you'd also lose Eli? And how come Eli was allowed to save me? I didn't get to choose. I thought the Watchers weren't allowed to interfere like that."

"Like I said, you were never meant to die at that time. In original history you live a long, healthy life."

"Do I? How long?"

Zac shook his head. "Eli told me how curious you are. I've told you enough about your future, I cannot tell you more. Suffice it to say, when Eli saved you, he was not altering history but putting it right again."

I let that sink into my brain, which was officially on overload, but I had more questions.

"But he was still altering his own history, he was never meant to have that accident."

"A brief stay in hospital does not vastly alter his future."

"It would have if he'd died."

"Although he is stronger than you, and judged more likely to survive, there was still that risk and that's why it had to be his decision."

"And he chose to save me."

"Yes."

Wow, that's mental. Does he care about me that much?

Once I'd allowed that mind-blowing fact to sink in, the questions resurfaced in my overloaded brain. "I thought you only had teenagers working for you but you said past Fixers helped him."

"Teenage Fixers grow up and go on to live normal lives with normal jobs but occasionally we ask them for help. We don't send many out on missions as we find adult targets are less likely to be open to advice from others, especially strangers. We also never recruit adults as they struggle with the concept of time-travel and, even if they did accept it, they would be opinionated, wanting to do their own thing. It is much easier to call on our ex-Fixers, who know how we work; they lend a hand when needed."

"Why don't they keep doing missions?"

"As I've said, adults are more difficult to steer in the right direction, I believe Eli told you, we did have someone try and guide Emma's father but it didn't work out. Also, if they work for us too long, they start to look much older than they should."

"What? Being a Time Fixer makes you age faster, nobody told me that!" My hand instinctively went to my face, feeling for wrinkles.

Zac smiled. "No, it doesn't, but think about it. Each time you go on a mission, you are gone for an hour, maybe two. On the way back we reset time for you but we can't reset your bodies. When you return, no time has passed for anyone else but, one or two hours have passed for you. If you continued doing missions all your life, years would pass for you that would not have passed for your friends. You would finish up being years older than them."

I stared at him, something in there made sense but I couldn't figure out what. I was really going to have to pay more attention in science or watch more sci fi programs. Enough mind bending, I needed more realistic answers.

"What happened to Kian, Liam and Ashley?"

"They are fine. Kian was returned home. Liam had been searching for him. When he heard what happened, he became very protective of his little brother. All the boys became very close. The original abduction of Kian never happened; Liam watched him too closely. All grew up healthy, lived their lives, had families etc."

It seemed strange to hear Zac talk about them in the past tense when all he was saying had still to happen.

"What families do they have?"

"Irrelevant. I wasn't told that much and I didn't ask. Their living made some impact on the future but for the better. It seems their traumatic experience influenced them to make good choices in the future. Kian became a police officer, Ashley, a doctor and Liam, a charity worker, raising money for needy children."

"That's amazing!" I shook my head, struggling to take in the massive change in their lives. "So, tell me about Lisa and Jake."

"They were charged. Jake's was a lesser role so he was given a supervision order for a year. After that, I would like to say he straightened out but, unfortunately, he continued to make wrong choices. Lisa, on the other hand, was put into secure accommodation for several years. When she was released, she returned to her Time Agency family."

"What happens to her? Couldn't she be returned to her past family, that's what she wants."

"Her Time Agency family cared for her well and made many steps to help heal the hurts within her. While she was 'locked up', they received counselling training and were a great help to her. She never caused any more problems for the Agency. She could never return to the past as that family died in the fire; she would have been alone and would not receive the help she needed. Even if that were not the case, it isn't possible to send back someone with so much knowledge of the future, especially someone like Lisa. Not to mention the difficulty in explaining where she had been for eight years. She was a young child when removed."

That made sense.

"Why was Lisa chosen to be a go-between? She's not exactly nice."

"Ah, but she was. Unfortunately, Lisa is an experiment that went wrong. She was a sweet little girl, as far as records showed and statements after the fire confirmed. Everyone said her death was a great loss, along with her parents. As she originally died, and was such a lovely child, the Watchers gave her a chance to live. It was a mistake, which won't be repeated. They didn't realise how much she resented their interference. She had everyone fooled. We only know of her bullying from you, she kept everything off-line and behaved perfectly for all adults so no problems were recorded. It was only when you stopped her, and the police were involved, that official reports were filed and, once the resulting waves reached them, the Watchers were able to see that Lisa was involved."

"I know waves started as soon as she took Kian, changing history, but couldn't the Watchers wait until the waves settled then send someone back to stop her before she took him?"

Zac smiled. "Not if time travel was eliminated. As soon as glimpses of that possible outcome came through the Watchers had to act immediately even though, at that stage, they had only patchy information."

"Oh."

"Her actions have upset the Watchers; they would love to help everyone but it isn't possible, they are a small organisation which they are trying to keep secret. They agonise daily on who to help. For one of their own to cause this much trouble is a huge shock for them. They want to continue but need to re-examine all their procedures. I'm sure there are lengthy discussions ahead."

"They won't stop the project though, will they? It's doing too much good."

"I doubt they will stop altogether, it means too much to them and, after-all, it did work out well with Kian's family, in the end, but it was a near disaster. Several lives were almost lost and Eli was seriously injured. They want to save people not cause them injury or death."

"But that was Lisa who caused it, not them, and you've said they'll not make the same mistake again. Can't they just continue with their existing Fixers and go-betweens?"

"That is one option they will consider; we will have to wait and see. Now, despite the debate, there is something they would like you to do immediately."

"What?"

"The reason I had to be the one to come see you is because they need you to do another mission and it has to go ahead now to prevent further time waves."

"Is it to do with Kian?"

"No."

"Then, why can't Eli explain when he's better? Why can it only be you?"

"Remember that I said if you died, we would also lose Eli?"

I nodded.

"Well, now I'll explain why. As you now know, the Eli who visits you is from two years in the future. In your time, Eli doesn't yet work for the Time Fixers. He is six months younger than you, he turned fourteen in January. Eli is making a mess of his life; he needs your help to change and we need you to recruit him to the Agency, just as the future Eli recruited you."

"Eli kept saying there were things he couldn't tell me as it would alter both our futures."

"Quite so. Your lives are linked. Right now, your task is to save the present-day Eli so that you and the future Eli may help many others. This is why the future Eli cannot come back to see you. It would get too confusing for you to see both of them at the same time. Also, we cannot risk both of them meeting."

"That would lead to a paradox, thingy?"

"Yes."

"But Eli already works for the agency, so I've already succeeded, haven't I?"

Did I actually just say that? How can I have already saved him when I haven't done anything yet?

"In your time, Jess, you have not yet saved him. There is no guarantee that you will be successful but if you fail, not only will Eli's life continue on its downward spiral but, all the people he helps in his role as a Time Fixer will be lost. You cannot fail."

***

CONTINUE THE STORY IN:

TIME FIXERS 2 – SAVING ELI

Coming soon

This is a work of fiction and is in no way based on any real person or situation.

If you have been affected by any of the issues in this book, please seek further assistance.

Ring:

Childline: 0800 1111 to report any abuse or neglect.

The Samaritans: 116 123 if you feel you cannot go on and have suicidal thoughts.

If you are having problems at home or school, talk to the school councillor or your parents. Don't keep things to yourself, sharing helps. There are people ready to listen and help, please don't suffer alone.

ACKNOWLEGEMENTS

I would like to thank the 2018/19 year 6 pupils from New Pastures School, Mexborough for their cover ideas and wonderful sketches.

I would also like to thank the children of Links4Youth, Highwoods Community Base, Mexborough for helping me chose which cover to use.

Other Books by Gail Jones UK

Young Adult Fiction

Witness

Rachel Brooks Trilogy

Family Secrets
Family Fear
Family Missing

Coming soon:
Time Fixers 2 – Saving Eli

Children's Books

Toby Squirrel & Friends

Toby is Lost
Thief
Beaut
Fire

Coming soon:
Elle is Adopted

To Keep up with all the latest news:

Visit Gail's website:

<u>www.gailjonesbooks.org.uk</u>
website coming November 2019

Or check out her facebook page:

www.facebook.com/GailJonesbooksUK

Or follow her on twitter

www.twitter.com/gjonesfiction

Printed in Poland
by Amazon Fulfillment
Poland Sp. z o.o., Wrocław